Endorsements for The War Within

A challenging novel about war, politics and the Muslim world Teenagers mature during the course of dramatic events as they work through their grief, fears and need to belong. A most challenging novel.

Cecile Ferguson, Lollipops – What's on for kids

Rosanne Hawke brings to life memorable characters and a colourful and exotic setting in this fast moving adventure story, a real page-turner that grabs you by the scruff of the neck and drags you through the action. Full of suspense and intrigue, it's about faith, courage and friendship in the face of confusion, violence, grief and hostility. It's realistic, yet refreshingly optimistic, and thoroughly readable. I found it a satisfying and rewarding novel.

Kate Graham, Youth Express

This book should be compulsory reading for students studying politics or society based subjects.

Lesley White, teacher, Fiction Focus

[The War Within] is more than an adventure. Besides the issues of grief, culture and war, it explores the need for third culture kids to return to the place where they grew up, in order to fully adjust in adult life…Rosanne's observations of the TCK experience are profound.

Beth Wyse, TEAMworld

[All the elements of successful cinema are present in [The War Within]: the exotic location, a developing love story, a kidnap, death and fighting, even family reunion. A real breath of fresh air, another taste of the Aladdin story for me.

Lorraine Marwood, Alive Magazine

The War Within

Published by Rhiza Press
PO BOX 1519
Capalaba QLD 4157
Australia

© Rosanne Hawke, 2016

Cover Design by Production Works
Layout by Rhiza Press

First edition published by Albatross Books, 1996. Title: Re-Entry
Second edition published by Lothian books, 2003. Title: Borderland
Third edition published by Rhiza Press, 2016.

National Library of Australia Cataloguing-in-Publication entry

Creator:	Hawke, Rosanne, author.
Title:	The War Within / Rosanne Hawke.
ISBN:	9781925139877 (paperback)
Series:	Hawke, Rosanne. Beyond borders ; 2
Target Audience:	For young adults
Subjects:	Australians--Pakistan--Fiction
	Young adult fiction.
	Pakistan--Social life and customs--Fiction.

Dewey Number: A823.3

The War Within

Rosanne Hawke

rhiza press

To Lenore for making me write,
and the wolfchild for making it live.

1

Jaime

My seat belt snapped and I settled back with my iPad, barely listening to the flight attendant point out exit routes. I'd flown often as I'd lived overseas all my life. Instead, I flicked through my pictures on Facebook. A lot were photos Dad had taken when we lived in Pakistan. The ones of snow-topped mountains always tugged at my heart. So did pics of Chitral and the Kaghan Valley, so beautiful with flower fields, alpine lakes and rushing rivers. The pics of bazaars reminded me of how much fun they were. Dad had taken shots of multi-coloured spices lined up in hessian bags, shawls and carpets hanging outside for shoppers to admire. Then there were street vendors cooking tikkas, pakoras and curries my stomach craved for even now. I could feel Pakistan calling me home and I couldn't wait to experience it all again.

Not everyone was as enthusiastic about my return to Pakistan, as I was. The image of Kate's face when I told her where I was going in the holidays had been priceless. I wished I'd had my phone out ready to click. Her face had contorted into her favourite incredulous expression, her upper lip curling to the right and her teeth prominent like a horse's, ready to bite. 'How can you go back to Pakistan?' she'd spluttered. 'It won't be the same. Your friends won't remember you. Terrorists are bombing schools. You're so weird, Jaime Richards.'

Her words no longer hurt me as they would have when I first arrived in Australia a year ago. Her 'weird' didn't make me feel like I had a disease, just different, which I guess I was. Besides, she had only been put out because she'd wanted me to come to a beach party she was organising in the holidays.

'Come over when you're back,' was all she'd said after her face returned to its normal shape.

During the flight over I hoped with a fervent passion that Kate was wrong, that even with the conflict my friends hadn't changed. Jasper was still there in his last year of school. I paused, thinking about him. We had been good friends and yet he had never written. I couldn't understand why. Then there was Liana, who had been like a big sister to me, always seeming to see further than the rest of us. She'd be meeting me at the airport. And as for Pakistan—deep down I didn't believe a place like that could possibly change, not in a year, surely.

When I finally came to stand at the top of the flight deck ready to step down, the azan sounded from a hundred mosques, calling the faithful to worship and I realised what I'd missed the most about this place: that old magic, the unpredictable atmosphere that ancient lands of legend have. It wrapped around me, making me unable to think logically and I was lulled into believing everything was the same.

I breathed in a mixture of burning manure, curry spices, sandalwood and open drains. Even the air smelt as it always had. Then it struck me that I'd never really noticed these smells when I was living here. The thought gave me a twinge of uneasiness. What if things wouldn't be all that I'd thought they'd be? But as I hesitated between memory and dream, the airport mosque took up the call to afternoon prayers. I grinned, surprised by the relief I felt at the familiar wail. Just like usual, all those taped voices were not quite in tune.

Getting through customs was more of an ordeal than I remembered. There were intimidating guys in blue with assault rifles slung over their shoulders, ordering me to open my bags. Their limited English made them sound suspicious, as if they thought I had bombs or drugs in my bag. I couldn't help but be apprehensive: what if someone had sneaked a package into my carry-on while I was dozing?

'What is in this bag?' One of the guards was holding up my cosmetics purse. How embarrassing. There were all sorts of 'unexplainables' in there. I gulped down my fear, trying to answer all their questions in the Urdu I'd learnt as a kid, and suddenly they couldn't do enough for me. I think the close-to-tears catch in my voice may have helped. Pakistani guys tend to fall into an over-helpful heap when they see women or children upset. Visible tears work better than a bribe every time.

'So, you are growing up in Pakistan? Accha, this is good. You are missing Pakistan, ji? That is why you visit us again?'

I nodded left and right, trying to put on just the right smile; demure enough to satisfy them that I was respectable, yet polite enough to encourage them to let me through without any trouble. The line behind me grew longer.

'Welcome home, missahiba.' The official finally handed me my bag. I must have looked puzzled for he kept talking and tipping his head as I took it.

'You are growing up in this country, this being your home

now. Khush amdeed, welcome.'

I made for the exit. Was he right? I'd just spent the whole year making Australia my home. But I couldn't think much about it then as the next problem loomed in view.

Outside were thousands of men. Maybe that's a little exaggerated, but it felt like that many—and they all seemed to be staring at me as I emerged from the terminal. I ducked my head, wishing I had a burqa to cover all of me. I was wondering how I'd get through the crowd when I heard my name.

'Jaime!' It was the closest I'd ever heard Liana come to a screech.

What a relief. Mr Kimberley, my music teacher, was there too. They'd been right in the front the whole time, but were lost to me in that ocean of faces. Mr Kimberley even hugged me while all those men watched our every move, open-mouthed. I tried not to feel embarrassed. Mr Kimberley had always been the super caring teacher, knowing what your problem was before you'd even worked out you had one.

All the way up the two-thousand-metre climb to the mountains, where the school was, we kept up a steady stream of questions and answers. Considering how quiet I remembered Liana to be, she kept up with me well.

'What are you doing now, Li?' I asked.

'Teaching English for the moment at the Urdu speaking school for girls, near ours.'

'You used to take me for walks down there. Remember?'

'When I was your "big sister" in Year 6 and you were still in Year 3. You were cute, but you had a mind of your own.'

'And you'd take me down to the woods and dance with me. With your dark hair and olive skin you looked like a

4

Bollywood dancer. I thought you'd be world-famous.'

'Funny how things turn out differently from what you think.'

'Yeah.'

When we reached my favourite part of the road that gave the best view of the mountains, I asked Mr Kimberley to stop. He parked the van and we all piled out, while I wrapped my shawl around me to keep out the cold. I stood at the bent iron safety rail—that realistically wouldn't have stopped a rusted bicycle from plunging over the edge—and soaked in the vision of the Kashmir Mountains. Snow covered their tops, blinking like quartz in the winter sun, and the mountains behind rolled back into each other like waves. It was unending and I felt as I had in childhood whenever we stopped there: forever secure, as though there were some things that would never change.

'We used to call this "Richards' Point",' I said. It was the sort of memory that drew tears; a bright spot of childhood tempered with the knowledge that those you had originally shared it with weren't present. There was a silence, then I felt Liana's arm come around me. 'I'm jolly glad you're here, Jaime.'

I grinned at her as we headed for the van. Since I had been in Australia a year, her way of talking, even though she, too, was Australian, seemed so outdated. Guess I must have sounded like that last year. No wonder I got teased.

Other than the snow and sculptured snowmen, the main thing I noticed at the school was the armed guards at the gate. Then I saw Ayesha. She'd spent hours teaching me and Liana local dances in the dorm after lights out when we were young, and she was already at the front door of the hostel as we pulled in. 'It is so good to see you, Jaime!' She was so excited she was squealing. I'd never seen her like that. She'd always been so demure and calm. I had no doubt that between her, Liana and Mr Kimberley, I had been missed.

'Great to see you too, Ayesha,' I managed to say before she squashed me in a hug that left me so breathless I wheezed. I could smell the scent of jasmine and mustard oil in her hair and it took me back more than the year I'd been away. She'd always smelt like that.

'It's great to be here.'

'Come upstairs where it's warm.' Carolyn met me on the stairs. She was still as exuberant as I remembered, red pigtails flying as she made plans. 'I've got a bed ready for you. Aunty Donna said you could sleep with Ayesha and me and the others in the dorm. Just like we used to. You can even come to school with us if you like.'

I almost said, 'Hey, this is my holiday,' but I thought it would be fun, being part of it all again. That must sound weird, but school there went on through January and finished in their summer, in July. We had studied at home during winter if the school was snowed in. Carolyn and Ayesha were only halfway through Year 11.

'Yeah, that'd be cool. Count me in.'

Carolyn grinned but Ayesha made some comment about it being cool enough as it was.

'Bet Jasper can't wait to see you, either,' Carolyn added. 'He's not here because of basketball practice. The inter-school tournament's this week.'

'How is Jasper?' I wondered what he'd be like now. We'd always been close ever since we compared scabs in Year 1. Liana's face suddenly closed as if she wished the topic of conversation would change, and Ayesha looked as if there was gossip to be told but didn't want to be the one to do it.

Part of me wanted to sit still and think, and filter all the data coming in, but Carolyn was laughing and pulling me up the stairs. Maybe I imagined that expression on the others' faces when Jasper's name came up. The excited part of me took over and I scrambled up the two flights of stairs after Carolyn, puffing at the top.

'Phew, they never knocked me out like this before.'

'That's because you haven't done it for a year.'

Liana was behind me. 'Actually, it's most probably the altitude. Better take it easy for a day or two.'

Carolyn was still pulling at me. 'Come on, here's the dorm.'

From the speed Carolyn made it up the stairs, I should have guessed there'd be a surprise. Donna, the housemother, hugged me at the door. I couldn't explain how good it was to see her, considering she helped bring me up, but I think she understood.

Then I noticed the other girls. They were standing in the centre of the room, expectant looks on their faces. In front of them on a table was a huge cake with 'Welcome Home, Jamie' scrawled over it in garish pink icing just as the head cook had always done whenever it was anyone's birthday; just like he'd done for me every year since Year 1. I took a step forward to check the name; my eyes spelt out the incorrect word, J-a-m-i-e, , and in brackets, my Pakistani name, Jameela. A single sob escaped. I tried not to sniff and snuffle while I hugged all the girls.

'It was Faisal's writing on the cake that finally did it,' I admitted afterwards to Ayesha as we changed for bed. 'Ever since I was tiny, he'd always spelt my name as J-a-m-i-e, as if he thought my parents were the ones who got it wrong.'

'It is just like old times, Jaime. We're going to have so much fun. Does everything seem the same, like you have only been away a month?'

'I don't know. I feel weird. Some things have fitted, but everything's still not in its right place. I spent so long getting used to Australia. I mean, Faisal's cake really helped but at the airport today I was scared. And everybody in the waiting area looked like a mass of people with no identity. I don't remember ever feeling like that when I was living here. There are military guys everywhere, and the workmen are building the school wall higher, aren't they?'

Ayesha shrugged. 'It is a precaution only, because of the bombings in Islamabad and Swat. Don't worry. It will take a little time to get used to everything again.'

'Guess so, but I don't have much time to spare.'

عَلَی

'Mum, is that you? It took me ages to get through and I could lose the connection any—'

'Jaime, what a relief. Was it a good flight? Are you okay?'

'Sure, though things seem strange.'

'How do you mean?'

'I don't know. It seems changed from what I remember. It's a bit scary. But I've probably imagined it. How's everyone?'

'Fine. Here's Elly …'

'Jammie? Hi! Guess what?

'What?'

'My mouse with the black spot on her ear had babies last night!'

'That's—really nice, Elly.'

'And Blake Townsend sent you a postcard.'

'Really? What's it say?'

'He said, "Have a good time". He must have thought you'd get it before you left. Andrew said it came from the other side of the black tree.'

'Stump, black stump.'

'Here's Dad. Hey, Jammie? Can I sleep in your room sometimes?'

'I guess, but don't let Basil sleep in there, his fur sticks to my cushions—'

There was a crackling.

'Hello, sunshine.'

'Dad. I miss you already.'

'Me too, sweetheart. I wish I could have come with you.'

'Yeah, we'd have fun.'

'You bet. Did you get your money changed?'

'Yeah.'

'Jaime? On the news they said—'

'The news is always worse at home than what's happening here, you know that.'

'Be care—'

I sighed as Dad's voice broke up and disappeared. I couldn't get him back. So much for Himalayan phone coverage.

2

Jaime

The next day, Ayesha invited me down to the bazaar. I waited for her in the garden and breathed in the fresh, chilled mountain air. Pine trees covered the hills like thick carpet. Beyond were the awesome Kashmir Mountains, and to the left, the Hindu Kush that blocked the way to Afghanistan. I let out a deep sigh but forced my eyes to stay open. I didn't want to miss a second's glimpse of Himalayan glory.

'Magnificent, aren't they?' Ayesha sat beside me.

'I missed this so much. There's nothing like it in Australia. Not that I've seen, anyway.'

'What is it like in Australia?' We walked through the gates and past the armed guards.

'In Australia?' How could I describe it to someone like Ayesha who had lived here all her life?

'Is it all kangaroos and jungle and beaches?'

'N–no. Where I live, it's like any other city, I guess. But it's different from Pakistan—more orderly, clean. You can get fined for dropping rubbish.'

Ayesha made a face, the faint shadow of a grin showing.

'I'm not kidding. There are laws against discrimination too. So they say. Not as much unemployment as here, although they think it's bad. There are institutions for people with disabilities, as well as older people who have no one to look after them. No beggars. It's just so different.'

Ayesha's face changed; the grin had gone and in its place was an 'I want to see it' look. 'You must miss it. Why did you come back?'

'Because I miss it here too. There's a kind of excitement here, a close-to-earth, raw atmosphere. I'm not explaining it very well but it can get a bit clinical in Australia—in the city anyway—everything you want when you want it, how you want it. People can be so private, you could collapse in your front garden and the neighbour across the road mightn't notice. Just a different way of life; different way of looking at everything, I guess.'

'Is that why you took your nose pin out? It wasn't understood there?'

'Yeah.' I went quiet for a while. Seeing Ayesha wearing her nose pin, like most Pakistani girls, made me miss mine, but there was no point getting it done again. I sighed, then remembered Ayesha's face when Jasper was mentioned yesterday. 'Is Jasper okay?'

She didn't answer straight away. 'You'll see for yourself. Not long after you left his father died.'

'That's awful. Why didn't anyone tell me?'

'I'm sorry.' But she wouldn't say more about it.

Soon afterwards we were in the heart of the bazaar. I had been waiting for that moment for so long. There was nothing like a true bazaar in Australia. Yet while we were walking down towards the food vendors—where I'd walked every year of my life that I could remember—something was different. There was a tension in the air that, incredibly, Ayesha didn't notice. When I mentioned it she put it down to my being away so long and not remembering. Maybe I was able to see the change *because* of being away. She lived in it and it had sneaked up on her. The atmosphere was more like a village on the Afghan border than a quiet holiday resort in the mountains. Normally I loved that excitement, the promise of adventure, but unexpected like that, it unnerved me.

I was quiet as Ayesha ordered kebabs. 'With chilli and lemon,' she added. We watched the vendor fan the coals with a woven straw fan as he put on the skewered meat. I noticed him glance behind him as he turned the kebabs and I was annoyed at myself that I couldn't enjoy the moment. He was the same vendor who'd always sat in that spot in front of the fountain and he remembered me, so why couldn't I relax?

Ayesha glanced at me. 'Don't worry, Jaime. When we bring people down here who haven't been to Pakistan before, they feel threatened and scared. You'll get used to it again soon.' She was trying to be helpful but it only made me worse. Why couldn't I feel at home?

Other vendors were calling out their wares. An old man in ragged clothes leading a donkey asked me if I'd like a ride. I shook my head, emotion threatening to rise over me like a wave, for he was the same man who'd taken me for rides when I was little. Women, swathed in long shawls or black burqas, babbled together about clothes and jewellery as they brushed past us and entered one of the many bangle shops on the street. Maybe I'd imagined the unease in the bazaar, after all.

Suddenly, I clutched Ayesha. I saw a group of men, Afghans, dressed in shalwar qameezes and huge wrapped turbans, carrying assault rifles over their shoulders. They were striding through the bazaar towards us.

'Ayesha! Look at them!'

'So? You know Pakistan. Men like that walk around everywhere.'

'But not here. Peshawar, maybe. They were never *here*.'

Ayesha shrugged. 'Maybe it's changed.'

'But Pakistan never changes.' Why did I say that? Guess I didn't want to admit things weren't the same. That's what had happened in Australia when I went back; everything had changed so much I couldn't fit in. Surely it wouldn't happen here too.

'Maybe not,' was Ayesha's exasperating reply and I didn't argue any more. Because of the Pakistani way of being polite, she wouldn't have realised she had contradicted herself.

The kebabs were ready. I took mine as I watched the men pass us. The kebab maker watched them too, then he leaned towards us.

'Girls, be going back to school now.' He said something else that I didn't catch. Ayesha nodded.

'What did he mean "go back to school now"?'

'Maybe you're right, Jaime. Let's go.'

'What is it? Ayesha?' But she was already moving along the street through the bazaar.

'This way will be quicker.'

'Ayesha!' I grabbed the end of her woollen shawl. 'Tell me what's going on.'

She stopped then, watching me as if to gauge what

my reaction would be. Then she shrugged. 'The man said he'd heard talk this morning in the bazaar. The militants are upset over a story in the paper. So it's best to go back to school.'

I understood and grinned. I just hated not knowing things.

'What are you smiling like a monkey for? It is important that we go now.'

We turned down a narrow alley—a short cut, she said—to the main road. I followed willingly, happy again. I'd been with Dad when bazaars had steamed up over an issue, usually at election time. He'd always delivered me home in time before anything serious had happened. One time when I was younger, when half the school was taken hostage, everything had turned out in the end. Even now I enjoyed the anticipation of excitement and the knowledge that I'd relish later: that I'd been there. Of course, I never wanted to see anything violent or dangerous.

We were almost out of the alleyway. Shopkeepers were standing at their doorways as if waiting for the end of the world and all the women had vanished. Ayesha was walking fast like a speed walker in the Olympics. I was about to tell her to slow up when I heard a shout. It took me a moment to realise it was in English. It sounded like my name. Ayesha must have heard it too for she stopped. In one of the shop doorways a Westerner was beckoning us.

'It's Uncle Jon! C'mon, Ayesha.' She seemed to be in two minds and I knew what she was thinking: that we should hurry to the school where it was safe.

'Jaime, come here. You mustn't—' Uncle Jon's words were lost in a sudden burst of gunfire behind us. We didn't need any more encouragement to scuttle into the shop where he stood waiting.

'Uncle Jon! How come you're here? Aren't you based in Peshawar?' I was breathless and Ayesha was anxious; she didn't know that we'd be safest with him. He was my father's best friend and had always treated me like his own daughter.

'Sure. But your parents wrote me and I was coming up to the school to welcome you to Pakistan. Not much of a welcome, I'm afraid.' He motioned towards the doorway through which we could hear the shouting and automatic fire coming from the bazaar.

'What's going on? It was never like this here before.'

'Mujahideen, militants. The conflict in Afghanistan has spilled over to here now and many groups have headquarters and training camps here in the mountains.'

What had been going on all the time I'd been getting used to a different life 'back home'? Sure, there was a lot of news coverage about Afghanistan because of the war on terrorism, but I thought Pakistan had calmed down. 'What's going to happen? Why aren't these guys in Peshawar anyway?'

'Peshawar's a hotbox at the best of times. Besides they're close to the Kashmir border here. And, if the UN can't do something soon, it's anybody's guess how it will end up.'

'Shouldn't we get back to school?' Ayesha ventured into the conversation.

Uncle Jon smiled at her. 'I think you're safer here, at the moment. They're only fighting among themselves, but being on the street could land you a stray bullet. Besides, the police will stop it soon and I'll take you back myself.'

I was thoughtful on the way back to school. Pakistan

had always seemed exciting to me when I was younger, but something subtle had changed. Maybe it was because I was older; that I knew there was more behind things now like people hurting and issues at stake. Or maybe it was because of the year in Australia, where I'd learnt everyone should have a fair go and violence wasn't the way to get what you wanted.

At school, I answered all Uncle Jon's questions about Mum and Dad, Andrew and Elly, and what it was like in Australia. Then he got that fidgety look on his face he used to wear at Christmas when he had a gift he knew we'd like. He watched me as he dug into his pocket, his blue eyes twinkling. His eyes reminded me now of the Australian beach in summertime and when they twinkled like that, it was a sure sign of something good.

'I have a surprise for you, Jaime. To welcome you back.' And he laid a box in my hand.

I tried to appear surprised, but really, some people you can read like sign language. A rush of affection welled up inside me. I couldn't remember when Uncle Jon hadn't been a part of my life.

'Why don't you open it?' He was like a boy then, excitement mixed with nervousness. His fair moustache twitched, the lines at the corners of his eyes crinkled just before I bent my head to lift the lid. I had to gasp as I wasn't expecting what lay in the box. Nestled there was a gold bangle (and I mean real gold; I knew the difference) with intricate patterns etched on the outside, like walls of mosques, and 'Jameela' engraved on the inside in Urdu script.

I couldn't think of anything to say—an unusual turn of events, which he seemed to appreciate. 'Lovely, isn't it? A friend of mine from across the border made it.'

'Afghanistan?'

'Yep. We de-activated a mine near his house. He hadn't known it was there and it was where his children often played.' Uncle Jon pulled at his moustache and smiled at some memory. 'He was embarrassingly grateful.'

'Awesome. I love it.' It made me feel more secure again. Uncle Jon had always been my childhood hero. Maybe everything didn't have to change.

عـلـم

'Hi, sunshine.'

'Dad! How come you rang? I talked to you yesterday.'

'I was just thinking about you, sweetheart. Besides, it was a bit miserable getting cut off like that.'

'I saw Uncle Jon today. There was a riot in the bazaar.'

'A what?'

'Don't worry, Dad, it was nothing. You know what it's like here. '

'Be careful, Jaime. I should've gone with you. It may not be as safe as we thought.'

'I'll be okay. Honest. Everything's calmed down like it always does.'

'I'll keep in touch. Ring if you leave the area? Love you.'

'Bye, Dad. Love you too.'

3

Jaime

The next day I got roped into going to the sports tournament held in Islamabad. It was my friends who persuaded me in the end.

'What's the use of coming all this way to see us, if we all go on an excursion for a week?' Carolyn lamented. Liana was going to help out too, and there were plenty of jobs for me, they said. I could even play hockey if I wanted. I was surprised they weren't concerned about travelling so far when there were possible terrorists in the area. But for them, there was always some sort of conflict going on.

It was Jasper who convinced me, though. When I finally saw him again, I knew something was wrong. He just didn't seem to be the Jasper I remembered. As I watched him talk, I wished that when people wrote emails they'd write about everything and not assume another friend had filled in the details.

'I'm sorry I didn't know about your father, Jas. Ayesha told me yesterday.'

'It's okay, I should have written. I haven't done anything much, except sport, schoolwork. Even that hasn't been crash hot.'

I nodded in sympathy. He looked a shell of the old Jasper, like a pumpkin with all the seeds scraped out. Not only that, he seemed tense, as if he were on the edge of a cliff and one small push would throw him into the valley, thousands of metres below. I guess a lot of us had been scarred in some way by death. Carolyn's brother died a few years ago when we were taken hostage as kids during a terrorist attack. A few of our teachers had died too, but I'd never lost anyone close to me. I struggled to find the right words for Jasper. 'It takes a long time to get through something like that. Don't be too hard on yourself.'

'Yeah.' He answered as if he'd been told it before and it didn't help either time. The bitterness and distance in his tone shocked me for we had been close, but as I tried to find that common ground we used to share, he kept moving away. I think it was then that I determined to go to the tournament. I wanted to be friends with him again and I only had a few weeks.

It wasn't long before the rest of the school was waving to us as the Coasters swung out of the hostel gates onto the main road. Carolyn was hanging out of the window, red pigtails flying as she shouted goodbye to her friends, until Liana pulled her in. I had to smile as she asked for the 'Aussie lollies' I'd promised them for the trip. Sitting quietly in a bus for two hours appeared to be impossible for Carolyn, even at sixteen.

I heard Jasper talking with some of the guys in the back of the bus—or rather, they were talking with him. He didn't contribute much except to say what strategies might work best on the basketball court. I sat back and enjoyed the view through the window. For most of the trip the snow mountains were in sight and when we drove through villages, I saw groups of men sitting chewing pan or picking their teeth. Some watched us with lazy interest as we passed. The younger ones craned their necks to catch a glimpse of the 'foreign girls'. I grinned to myself; not much had changed after all.

The bus's horn blared then, warning a mangy dog off the road. I'd always liked the Coaster's horn; as a child I found it comforting. Now it reminded me of Australian trains.

When we arrived at the American school in Islamabad, it was much like walking into a high school in Australia, except for the armed guards standing at the gates. They reminded me of a war movie. The school was new—not like our buildings in the mountains that had been built during the Raj—and wherever we looked, we saw modern equipment and expensive furnishings.

'A lot of embassy kids go to this school,' Ayesha informed us. I hoped we weren't gawking. 'They can afford all these facilities.'

'How the other half do live,' was Carolyn's comment. She looked as though she'd say more but we shushed her as a few boys dressed in imported jeans burst out of a side room, brushed past us and headed off down the corridor. We followed them into a massive auditorium.

'Get a look at the polished floors in this place!' Carolyn said. 'Anyone would win a game with a place like this to practise in.'

An organised system of allotting billets was in progress. We saw Jasper walk off with an African guy and soon after, I heard my name and Liana's. A girl with brown hair similar to mine came forward to welcome us.

'Hi! I'm Sonya,' she said with an accent I couldn't place.

Liana introduced us and Sonya steered us to a car outside. What that car seemed like to Liana, I couldn't tell, but I'd just come back from the West and even I was impressed. It was one of those shiny black Mercedes that you only see at society weddings in Australia. In Pakistan, they have a flag flying on the bonnet.

'They've got to be embassy people,' I whispered to Liana. She didn't answer, trying not to seem impolite, I guess, but Sonya noticed my interest.

'You like our car? Then you may like our house as well.'

I smiled as I got in but I was embarrassed. Liana leaned over to me. 'Sounds a bit condescending?' It was my turn not to answer. Sonya seemed a little too knowing.

'So you are on the hockey team?' Sonya inquired from the front as the driver pulled out from the school parking area that was as big as a supermarket carpark at home. Liana nodded as I strained to hear. The distance between the front and back seat felt as wide as the hockey field we were discussing.

'So am I,' Sonya continued. 'Maybe we shall become such good friends, we shall allow each other to win.' We all giggled politely but I could tell by the look on Liana's face that she thought it as improbable as I did.

'Here we are,' Sonya announced after a short and fast ride through narrow tree-lined streets. I stared up at the two-storeyed Middle-Eastern-style house. What a country of contrasts Pakistan was. Yesterday in the bazaar there were people in rags selling bootlaces for a living and here was a house that would only be seen on the North Shore in Sydney. I tried not to stare too long at the white marble facade and the ornate archways that led off the upstairs balcony into many rooms beyond.

Sonya swept us into the house and up a carpeted staircase to our room. A bearer appeared from out of the air (almost) to carry our bags up after us.

'What a lovely room,' Liana said in the polite tone reserved for royalty. She was right about the room, though. I sat on the bed and studied the floor. There were rugs scattered everywhere; all special, one-of-a-kind rugs, mostly Afghan. Dad used to haunt carpet shops when we lived in Pakistan. He'd bought some excellent ones but not any as unique as Sonya's.

I offered a compliment. 'These are excellent rugs. Where did you get them?'

'Oh, we have friends.' Sonya answered so vaguely that it made me feel I'd been nosy. She crossed the room. 'Here is your bathroom and my room is the next one. That door between our rooms leads down steps to the garden.' We followed her gaze. 'It is usually best to keep it locked.'

I wondered why, but thought I wouldn't ask any more questions. My resolve didn't last long. 'You have a great house. Does your father work in an embassy?'

She hesitated, only slightly, but enough for me to wish I hadn't opened my mouth. 'Yes. You could say that. My father comes from Moscow.'

'Your mother is here?' Liana sounded tentative. I sympathised with her. It's awful when a person makes you feel as if you're walking on eggshells.

Sonya picked at the wool on her sweater for a moment. 'My mother died. In the Afghan war.'

'I'm so sorry.' I put my hand on her arm for an instant but she moved away.

'It happened years ago.' She looked down at her arm where I'd touched it, as if there'd be a mark. 'My mother was special.' Sonya sighed. 'But we will not speak about that now.'

There was a short silence. 'I would never have taken you for a Russian, Sonya,' I said. 'You've got such lovely olive skin.' I don't know why I said it. She'd unnerved me and I guess I was hoping to draw her out, to find that middle-of-the-road communication that can be found with a new acquaintance. Only it didn't work with Sonya. She stiffened as if I'd been offensive. I spoke quickly. 'I–I didn't mean to be rude.'

Liana glanced at me and I wondered what to do next when suddenly, just as if she'd pulled across a curtain, Sonya smiled again and said in a much lighter tone, 'It does not matter. Tell me now about you instead.' She sounded as if she'd just walked across a minefield into a safety zone. And I couldn't help wondering whether the enthusiasm she managed to drum up was contrived.

'That boy I saw with you in the auditorium, is he your brother? Or—'here she actually smiled '—is he your boyfriend?'

'Boyfriend?' Liana looked blank. 'Which boy?'

'The tall one, handsome, with dark hair, black leather jacket …'

Realisation dawned. 'Oh, you mean Jasper Pembley,' I said.

'Jasper,' Sonya said the name as if she were tasting it. 'What a strange name.'

'It's Pakistani. His parents were working here when he was born.'

Liana broke in then. 'He's not our brother; he's American and we're Australian.'

I couldn't say anything at that point. I was suddenly reminded of how much like a brother Jasper had been to me.

'He seems different.' It took me a moment to realise Sonya was still talking about Jasper. 'Sort of responsible, but troubled.' She sure didn't miss much.

'Poor Jasper's had a hard time,' Liana volunteered with a glance at me. 'Almost a year ago his father was killed in Afghanistan. He was a doctor and went in to help the wounded.'

'So!' Sonya's eyes lit up. 'A man with a cause.'

'It wasn't like that. He had no political preference when it came to the freedom fighters. He just wanted to help injured people.'

Sonya looked thoughtful. 'How very interesting. And what was the name of the place where he died?'

'No one knows,' Liana answered. 'He never said where he was going. It wasn't in his diary. Maybe that was to protect people involved. He probably wasn't supposed to be there when there was so much fighting. People have tried to find out what happened.' As I listened to Liana my heart ached for Jasper. The past months must have been hell for him.

'Maybe Dr Pembley walked on a mine,' Liana continued. 'Although most people believe the Taliban killed him. He was American, after all.'

'Yes, Afghans are very protective of their way of life. Some more than others. So, it seems we all have some trouble to bear at times. It must be difficult for this Jasper. At least I was able to go to my mother's funeral and grieve.'

'Not knowing is the worst,' Liana agreed. 'I don't think Jasper has come to grips with the reality that his father is dead at all.'

I'd been watching Sonya for this entire exchange, and although she'd been a bit weird at first, she did seem genuinely concerned about Jasper. That was when I noticed a strange look come over her face, as if she were about to make a comment, but changed her mind. Instead, she abruptly looked at her watch and moved to the door.

'We must get ready for the program tonight. I have asked Aslam to bring the car around the front in half an hour.' Then she smiled briefly at us and left.

'Whew. What do you think, Li?'

'She sure gives the impression we're not the most important thing in her life at the moment.'

I decided not to worry about it and unpacked my bag. That night I'd get to wear my Australian clothes again. No dupattas or shalwar qameezes would be worn at the American school, that was for certain.

علم

'Hi. Mum?'

'Jaime, lovely to hear you.'

'I'm in Islamabad. Dad said to ring if I went anywhere.'

'What are you doing down there?'

'Sports tournament. They've got it in January this year. So I came too. Is Dad there?'

'He took Andrew to the Adelaide oval for the opening of the test series. Your father thought he should be educated—see the toss of the coin and all that. Besides, it's Pakistan playing. By the way, Kate Sample rang to see what you were doing. Something about a beach party. Didn't you tell her you were going away?'

'Yeah, but she's on another planet half the time. She probably thought I was back already. Mum, can you tell Dad that Jasper Pembley's father is presumed dead. They were friends, weren't they?'

'Oh no. How's the boy doing?'

'Not good. It's changed him. We used to get on so well. A lot's changed here, actually.'

'Give him time, Jaime, and yourself too. It must be like coming back to Australia last year.'

'Guess so. Look, Mum, I'll ring again. To catch Dad. Okay?'

'All right, darling. Bye.'

4

Jaime

The American Teen Centre was a blur of rock music, gyrating bodies, and imported food and drink. It was even more Western than the Year 12 dinner at my school in Australia— which was strange in the heart of a Muslim country. It was like the kids acted more Western than they needed to be, in case they forgot who they were. One guy near me was saying how sick his drink was. Kate Sample used to use words like that but I was still behind the times.

Jasper wasn't in the mood for dancing and we were almost through our Baskin Robbins ice creams (shipped in fresh from the U.S.) when Sonya approached us, looking as if she'd lost her phone. A strange impulse always made me want to say things to make people feel better, but with Sonya it always came out making me sound like a child.

'Is anything wrong?' I tried to appear as mature as Liana but Sonya answered me in the exasperated tone that people reserve for three-year-olds who interrupt adult conversations.

'I have just received word …' she began, then started afresh as if she remembered we weren't worthy of her news.

'I have to see someone.' She sounded professional then, her earlier hesitation done with. 'It is quite important. I shall need to take the car, so you had better come with me. We can go home from there.'

None of us answered. It sounded unorthodox, taking us away from a program arranged especially for all the participating schools. I was sure that if we'd asked a teacher, we'd be denied permission and I wasn't sure how to say that without appearing a wimp. She must have sensed my nervousness for she smiled suddenly.

'I am sorry we have not been here long.' She said it with one eyebrow raised and a smile that didn't win me over. Nor did she look as if she'd listen to any excuses and suddenly I couldn't be bothered arguing about it.

I glanced at Liana. She nodded. 'Okay,' I agreed.

Jasper surprised us then. 'I'd like to come too. I told my host I would go back to his place by myself. I've been here enough times before.'

Sonya turned her gaze on him. From my angle I could see her eyes; they were gold—I hadn't noticed before—and wide open. Guess she was as surprised as I was.

'Can you speak enough Urdu to keep out of trouble?' she asked with just enough lift of her eyebrow to imply she didn't expect him to speak anything other than English. None of the kids from the American school seemed to have any cultural awareness at all.

'Sure. And Pakhtu.'

'So? And how did you learn that?' Interest flamed in Sonya's face as she looked up into his and I suddenly saw him as she might. I'd never noticed before how attractive he was (that is, when his 'half on, half off' grin was showing). And I could see what she meant about that 'uniqueness' she'd mentioned earlier; an element of 'something stirring under the surface' that intense guys often have.

'I was brought up in Peshawar,' was all he said, and suddenly Sonya turned as if she were the lead girl in a marching group, and we followed her out to the car. Sonya slid into the front seat next to the driver and I sat in the back seat, watching the bazaar night life flashing past too fast. I marvelled at how she could travel around the city at night when all good Muslim girls were safe at home in purdah.

Sonya seemed weirder that night—if that were possible. She didn't make any conversation as she usually did, and before the driver had even put the brake on at our destination, she was out of the car, clutching her bag.

'I shall not be long,' she called as she pulled a red woollen shawl around her shoulders and turned towards the shops.

'She should have taken us with her.' Liana sounded concerned and I knew what she was thinking.

'Yeah, no girls walk around here alone at night. That hasn't changed, has it?'

It was Jasper who answered me. 'No, it hasn't.'

'Then what can be so urgent that it can't wait for tomorrow?'

None of us shared anything. Jasper looked as if he had a few thoughts about it that he didn't like.

'I'm out of here.' And he heaved his long legs out the door.

'Where are you going?' I hated to sound so shrill, but I didn't feel like being left in the bazaar with a driver who we knew nothing of, except that he drove too fast. Apparently

Liana felt the same. She was a step ahead of me, though.

'I don't think you should follow her, Jasper. She mightn't appreciate it.'

'Don't sweat; I won't be long.' He actually grinned as he sauntered off, his hands in his jacket pockets.

'That's the brightest I've seen him since I've been back,' I murmured.

Liana didn't answer; we both leaned forward, watching him casually walk along the narrow street as if he were window-shopping. The sweepers hadn't come yet to clean the streets and the day's rubbish still littered the narrow pavement. A dog with only one ear slunk past the car, sniffing the ground and nosing over long-life milk cartons. Only a few late male shoppers strolled by, talking and laughing.

Jasper stopped at a narrow Afghan rug shop, staring in the window as if he had ten thousand rupees to spend. Then he slipped inside. That was when the horn suddenly blared. The driver had drifted off to sleep and slumped onto the wheel.

'Great. A sleeping driver, no guy and Sonya nowhere to be seen.' That might sound like feminine helplessness in Australia but in Afghanistan, you could get arrested for not having a male escort. Even a ten-year-old little brother could make a girl respectable—without one, she was nothing.

5

Jasper

Inside the shop, Jasper could hear voices speaking earnestly in Pakhtu. The sound came from up a flight of narrow wooden stairs.

'Za! Go! The car horn! That is the warning. You must not delay, Sonya,' came a deep voice. 'What could be wrong?'

'Don't worry. It is most probably one of the kids I brought with me.'

The man made a popping sound like a shaken bottle of soda imploding. Even Jasper took a step backwards. 'You did what? Why do such a foolish thing?'

'I am sorry, Uncle jan. I had to. I am looking after them. It is a pity I have to at a time like this, but they are only school kids and you did say to do everything as normally as possible.'

Jasper was startled to find Sonya could speak Pakhtu. He knew she was Russian, so how did she learn it?

His eyes were used to the dim light in the shop by then; it seemed to be closed for the night, but he could still see the rich red colours of the rugs hanging on the walls and covering the floor. More rugs were rolled and stacked along one wall like hundreds of cells in a beehive. Cushions made of carpet were set against the other walls for customers to lounge against while they argued about the price and drank green tea. Striking blue lapis and silver jewellery was displayed in a glass cabinet.

Jasper fingered the beads on a woven donkey bag. The voices upstairs were lower now and he couldn't pick out the words. He glanced around the dim room and his eyes were drawn to a spot on the wall above him. He could only just make it out in the low light. It was an old photo in a silver frame. The tall, burly man holding a Kalashnikov AK 47 was a Pakhtun, but the one with him was a Westerner; the fairer hair gave him away instantly. Surely not. Jasper leaned up against the wall, straining for a better look. His breath came in a gasp. 'Dad!'

'Za, Sonya.' The voices were at the top of the stairs. 'I shall see you tomorrow, or before, if I can manage it.'

Stunned as he was, Jasper knew he mustn't be found in the shop. He quietly let himself out, and with a contrived appearance of nonchalance, he gazed into the next shop window.

Sonya emerged from the doorway and saw him instantly. 'What are you doing?' Her voice was sharp. 'I told you to stay in the car.'

He took a deep breath and turned casually to face her. 'These are excellent rugs,' he said.

She softened slightly. 'I needed to do some business for my father and I don't want to worry about you loose on the street.'

'He sells rugs?' Then he forced himself to say, 'I'm sure my father would have been interested in these.'

Sonya hesitated, but only a moment. 'We'll return now.' She led him back to the car.

6

Jaime

Liana and I watched Sonya and Jasper talking outside the shop before they returned to the car. When Jasper threw himself in the back seat beside me I didn't need telepathy to know there was something wrong. He said nothing but breathed heavily as though he was running a race inside his head, and if he didn't win, a catastrophe would occur.

Jasper was dropped off at the house with us and as Liana walked in with Sonya, I stayed outside hoping he would tell me what happened. I'd always been taught to talk about what's bothering me, and Jasper's obvious hurt and his quietness broke me up. I knew he wouldn't share anything unless I started the ball rolling.

'Jasper, what was in the shop? Sonya was in there, wasn't she? Did she see you then?'

He shook his head. 'She doesn't know I was inside—'

'What happened?' The look on his face wasn't encouraging. At first I thought he would shrug and return to his host's house, but then an 'oh what the hell' look came over his face and he began to talk at last. He told me about the shop, the voices, Sonya knowing Pakhtu (which seemed to bother him a lot) and the photo.

'The guy could have picked it up in a second-hand shop, but perhaps he knew Dad.' He moved his arms as if to keep warm and his pacing practically wore a circle on the pavement.

'Maybe I should have said I was there. It could have been all above board. Maybe I could have asked. But when I heard them coming down the stairs I had this feeling that something wasn't right.'

I didn't know what to say. He was too upset and I knew that whatever I said, he'd take it the wrong way. Instead, I simply nodded to keep him talking.

'And Sonya—what's she up to anyway? Drives around in a Russian embassy car, her father's away and yet she goes to an Afghan rug shop and is on friendly, and I mean cosy, terms with the guy there.'

'That's weird. Afghans wouldn't be that close to Russians. Even though it's years since they moved out, memories are long.'

'So, what's with her, I wonder. She's as cool as a house shut up for winter. She hardly flinched when she found me outside the shop. Said she was doing business for her father.'

I found myself staring at him in pity. Even then I thought of Sonya as a regular girl. Maybe her father had bought a rug and she had made a payment for it. But I knew I couldn't say that to Jasper. It was as if the negative feelings he held inside needed to be justified and pinned onto another reason. He was using Sonya as a scapegoat and his comments seemed to confirm that, yet it gave no satisfaction. It only left me with the unfulfilled urge to hug him and make him better.

As he turned to go to his host's house, he looked back at

me and I caught my breath at the tortured look on his face. 'I knew he wasn't thinking about the carpet shop any more. 'God, Jaime. I wish I knew what happened to Dad.'

ↄᎾↄ

The next morning I couldn't concentrate on anything Liana said at breakfast. I kept worrying about Jasper and playing with my food.

'All ready for today?' Sonya whisked in. Her voice pulled me out of my reverie.

'Yeah,' I answered dutifully. 'Just have to finish getting ready.' I paused. 'Do you have a spare hairclip I could borrow for the hockey game?'

She took the clip out of her own hair and handed it to me. It was blue lapis lazuli with a silver fastener, a French one that popped open when the clasp was squeezed. I was flabbergasted. 'This is too good for playing hockey.'

I was meaning to be polite but she sounded annoyed when she answered me. 'Think nothing of it. You are my guest.'

That was when she noticed my bangle. 'How beautiful.' She stretched out a finger and rubbed it along the carving on the outside. It was the first time I'd seen her reach out in any way to either of us.

'My uncle gave it to me.'

'It was my uncle who also gave me this clip. Please wear it. This is my wish.' Her tone had totally changed and as she stood there looking at me, I had the strangest impression that we had something in common, but I couldn't think what it was.

Just as Liana and I stood to go upstairs, Sonya became business-like again. 'There is important information you should know.' I paused wondering what she'd say. 'There has been talk of a prowler in the area. It would be better not to go outside at night alone.'

'Is he dangerous?' Liana asked.

Sonya bit her lip. 'I'm sure it's nothing to be worried about, but best to be warned.'

All through the day at the school campus, while we played matches, the American kids were 'putting on the dog' for us: feeding us Coke, genuine (and non-halal) hot dogs and Baskin Robbins ice cream. We ended up losing the last hockey match and I also lost Uncle Jon's bangle. I was devastated when I realised and ran back onto the oval searching for it.

Sonya found me there. Her congenial mood of the morning had worn off. When she spoke to me she sounded exasperated. 'Don't you know it is getting late? We must return home.'

'I'm sorry, I lost my bangle. The clasp mustn't have been shut properly ...' Tears were close.

She held out her hand. 'This is what you search for?'

On her palm was the bangle. 'Where did you find it?'

'A girl was taking it to lost property and I recognised it.' Sonya made a comment about my Pakistani name being Jameela but it didn't sound sincere. What I did find weird was how she even knew my other name. I hadn't told her and it was written in Persian script on the bangle. She couldn't have understood that, could she?

Later that evening I stood at the window, staring through the twilight at the Margala Hills. Two days we'd been there and I still hadn't worked out what sort of person Sonya was. At breakfast she was the kindest she'd ever been. She'd let me keep the clip in my hair and even borrow her red shawl to wear to the movie that the Teen Centre was showing that night. I couldn't put my finger on what didn't add up and I imagined Mum telling me to be careful.

I wondered what my family were doing at home. Dad had so wanted to come with me. To keep me safe, he had said, just in case the terrorism was as bad as Australian media portrayed it. Money was the problem, of course. It was Grandad's bonds which paid for my ticket. Dad would have loved seeing the bazaar and the carpet shops again. Thinking of Dad never failed to lighten my spirits. He had such a sense of fun and adventure, even if he did find it hard to settle back in Australia. He fitted in so well in Pakistan; with his dark hair and beard and dressed in a shalwar qameez, he looked just like everyone else.

My thoughts turned to Jasper then. Did he smile as I just had when he thought of his father? I didn't think so. Yet, I knew it shouldn't have to be like that. Couldn't he remember the good times and enjoy those, be thankful he had them? Before I left Pakistan I used to think Jasper was resilient, as though he drew strength from beyond himself and had an internal transformer to make it his own. Now it was as if he'd cut off his whole life-support system and it was a struggle for him to breathe.

The call to evening prayer from the mosque broke into my thoughts. It was seven by my watch and dark outside. We wouldn't be leaving for another half-hour. Liana was still in the shower. No one would notice if I slipped out to sit on the balcony for a while. The evening air was crisp and misty, reminding me of girls in long scarves dancing in a forest.

Carefully I opened the outside door and stepped out onto the balcony. I heard the click behind me and groaned. No wonder Sonya told us to keep the door locked; it was one of those that shut by itself. I didn't have my phone to ask Liana to open it. Now I'd have to go all the way around the front to get back in, and there was no light. It was colder than I realised too. I clutched the handrail as I carefully stepped down to the garden. The grounds were immense; I hadn't had a chance to explore them. I was attracted by the sound of the fountain and kept walking further from the house. I could just make out its shape. Dad would have loved it, for it was shaped like the minaret of a mosque. Water came splashing out where the loudspeaker would have been.

Then Sonya's warning about a prowler came to mind. I glanced around. I couldn't see far. Nor could I hear anything, other than the splashing of the water. Maybe Sonya did have cause to warn us, I should have remembered. My unease swiftly turned to icy prickles that ran up my back and the hair separated on my head. Someone was behind me, I was sure of it, yet I was too scared to check. The house seemed so far away. The wall and dark hedge by the road were too close for comfort.

I hurried over the lawns towards the house, praying I'd been mistaken, my heart thumping too fast. Then I heard the breathing behind me, footfalls keeping up with mine. I tried to move faster, but it was like a bad dream where I couldn't move, and the unseen threat loomed. When I screamed it was soundless.

Suddenly I was jerked backwards by a heavy weight on my shoulder. I froze, but only for a moment. I took in breath, ready to shout, but a hand clamped over my mouth. A man's voice whispered, 'Raza! Raza!' and other stuff I couldn't catch. He didn't sound psychopathic but I wasn't taking any chances.

I breathed out deeply from my stomach and tried to calm down. Instantly, the hand was removed from my face and I twisted and kicked out as hard as I could. The man gasped and let go of my shoulder. I flung my arms up and felt my fingernail rip through smooth flesh. He grunted and, in that second, I could smell the same woolly smell of Dad's Afghan carpets as the man let me go.

I didn't need another moment to think. This time I turned and ran, panic giving flight to my feet, but it wasn't fast enough. The guy must have thrown himself after me and the impact flung me to the ground with him half on top. At that point, images flashed through my mind; stories I'd been told of girls attacked in the night, disgusting things that we'd whispered about in boarding school with a thrill of horror. I groaned. God, help me. I never thought it would happen to me.

The man's hold on me was much tighter this time as he pinned me to the ground. I tried to say, 'No', but it came out as a whimper. I looked up and saw the dark outline of the house, closer now. I struggled to get free but the man was too strong.

Just as I was about to scream something smashed into my head. At first I was stunned, until pain ripped across my mind, jagged and red. Then there was nothing.

7

Jasper

Jasper rang the bell on the outside gate of Sonya's house and was ushered into a foyer by a servant, who soon rushed off to find the girls. He stood there admiring the rugs on the floor and on the walls, wondering if they came from the shop. Each one was Afghan and some were ancient. He ran his finger along the border of a threadbare one and frowned. It had been repaired but the old pattern seemed to be changed along the border.

'Jasper! Am I glad it's you!' Liana rushed towards him, Sonya not far behind her.

He turned towards Liana with a smile. 'I came to take you all to the movie—'

It was as if she hadn't heard him. 'We can't find Jaime.'

'Hey, wait up a minute. Is this the cool and calm Liana?'

'Jasper, listen! There's a prowler and—'

'You lost me. Why can't you find Jaime?'

'I don't know,' Liana answered, quieter now. 'Sonya warned us not to go into the grounds at night. But you know what Jaime's like. When I got out of the shower, she was gone. She wouldn't think twice about walking outside and sitting in the dark.'

Jasper turned to Sonya. 'What the hell is going on?'

Sonya didn't even flinch. 'I cannot help it if they are so stupid to go outside after I have warned them about the danger.'

Jasper opened his mouth to speak, glanced at Liana and thought better of it.

'Don't you think we should get help?' Liana looked from Jasper to Sonya, but Jasper just stared at Sonya, his face darkening. Why wasn't Sonya calling for a search party?

Liana asked, 'What about the police?'

Sonya cast Liana a withering glance, but Jasper was immune to scornful looks.

'When did you first hear of the prowler?' he asked.

'Yesterday.'

'And you've searched?'

Liana cut in, 'She's not in the house and we were just checking outside when you came. The chowkidar hasn't found her, either.'

'I think Liana has the right idea, we should tell the police.' Jasper pulled out his phone and Liana moved to his side.

'No!'

Jasper looked up in surprise. Sonya's expression was so anxious all of a sudden that it made him wonder if maybe she was human after all.

'You know how the police can be here. They would take too long. They might ask for a bribe. We would never find her.'

'You have a better suggestion?' Jasper didn't bother keeping the sarcasm from his tone. He caught Liana glancing at him in concern.

'Actually, I do.' Sonya gave the ghost of a smile, which Jasper mirrored. Liana frowned at them both.

'We should go straight away. I know someone who can help.'

Jasper hesitated.

'I still think we should go to the police,' Liana said.

'It's true about the police, Li,' he said, then his mouth tightened. If Sonya was playing a game, he could play along. He turned to Sonya. 'After you.'

In the back of the car, Liana turned to Jasper, 'I wasn't expecting you to come.'

He answered quietly. 'You hadn't arrived at the Teen Centre yet, so I thought I'd check if everything was okay. I'm glad I did. I get the impression that finding Jaime is not high on Sonya's priority list. Besides, remember when I followed her last night?'

Liana nodded.

'I think Sonya's mixed up in something. The more I think about it, the more suspicious it seems.'

'Why do you think that?'

'The fact that she's Russian and knows Afghans and speaks Pakhtu.'

'How can that matter? The days are gone when Russians were a threat to the Afghans.'

'I'm not so sure. There's always talk of Moscow spreading out and controlling the Muslim states on the Afghan border again, especially with other militant groups growing in the Middle East. Everyone's after a slice of the pie.'

'But they're not Russia's states any more. That all finished with the Union breaking up years ago.'

'What about Ukraine? And they are still part of the Commonwealth, with Russian advisors influencing their governments.'

'You can't be serious.'

Jasper set his face and stared out the window.

'You are, aren't you?' Then she added, 'You have to let this go, there'll be no proof Sonya's—'

He shushed her as Sonya made a movement in the front seat. Then she turned to face them as the driver stopped the car.

'We have arrived,' she announced with an air of command that made Jasper give Liana a see-what-I-mean look. Liana blew out a breath.

'I shall go and see my friend.' Sonya moved to get out of the car, but Jasper was out his side door before both her feet had even touched the ground.

'I'm coming with you.' His jaw was firm and Sonya hesitated long enough for Jasper to relax. He knew he'd won.

She just shrugged. 'As you wish.'

Liana took one look at the dimly lit bazaar and joined them. Sonya graced them both with an expression that showed her frustration as she walked towards the carpet shop.

Jasper bent and whispered in Liana's ear. 'She's weird.'

'Your ideas are weird,' she whispered back. Then Jasper put his arm around Liana's shoulders. She glanced up in surprise at his sudden gesture of comfort. 'I was right, Li. This is the same carpet shop she went into last night.'

They looked at the rugs hanging in the window with others thrown over camel stools in a haphazard window design that made Jasper think of wild desert places and mountain tops. Sonya was the first to notice the heavy padlock. Her first few words were unintelligible. Then she muttered, 'They have gone already.' She looked so undecided and normal for a moment that Liana made a suggestion.

'If you don't want the police in on this, then we should go to the Australian Embassy.'

It was as if she hadn't spoken. Sonya seemed to have pulled herself together and was gazing at Jasper. 'Please,' she actually said, so that Jasper raised his eyebrows in disbelief. 'There is nothing to be concerned about. There is a person who will know where she is. We can travel there and get her back.'

Jasper didn't answer; just stood, staring at her.

'The decision isn't just up to you, Jasper,' Liana said. 'We need more information to decide.'

'I cannot tell you anything else.' Sonya was almost pleading. *Almost.* 'Just … trust me.'

Jasper laughed. 'That's the problem. I don't trust you.' He chewed his lip, and he thought of what he'd heard in the shop the night before. And the photo; how he'd love to quiz Sonya on that. He glanced up at her. She did look as if she knew where Jaime was.

'Okay. We find her ourselves. No police. No embassies.' Sonya closed her eyes as though she'd won and didn't want the victory to shine.

'But, Jasper. We can't …' Liana paused mid-sentence at the irritated scorn that settled again on Sonya's features. 'Think about this. You always decide things so quickly and now I have to go along with this stupid plan.'

But Jasper had been doing more swift thinking. 'Sonya,' he faced her squarely, so she could look nowhere else, except up at him, 'I don't leave your side. We're in this together. Understand?'

'As you wish,' was her only comment.

Jasper glanced down the bazaar. 'Right. Where is this person who can help?'

Sonya started back to the car. 'He will be on the road to Peshawar. We should hurry, before he realises …'

Jasper stopped short, feeling like he'd walked into an invisible wall. 'Peshawar! That's three hours away, and near the Afghan border. Are you crazy?'

'No,' Sonya flung back, her spirits obviously revived. 'But Jaime might be in trouble if we don't find her soon.'

Jasper fell into step beside Sonya. 'You didn't tell us about Peshawar.' He glanced at Liana but didn't like the 'I told you so' look on her face. *Peshawar.* How could he go there again?

'You did not ask.' Sonya was almost flippant as she stopped to face him. 'Besides, we cannot waste time arguing. We need to send Aslam to get an unmarked car. We would be too conspicuous in this one.' She moved on again. 'Also, we girls need to wear covering clothes for Peshawar. I presume you are coming?' The query was directed at Liana. 'We shall go to the house now. Jaldi!' This she threw at the driver as she flung herself into the front seat and the others climbed into the back.

'You're mad!' Liana managed to hiss at Jasper. 'How will we find Jaime in a wild place like Peshawar?' Jasper couldn't answer. He was staring out the window, feeling as hopeless as he had that day at school, all those months ago, when the news had come from Peshawar that his father was missing, presumed dead in Afghanistan.

8

Jaime

In my dream we were all standing round the piano and Mum was clowning around, playing a blues version of 'Für Elise'. It was a family gathering that no one else would find remarkable, but to us, it was hilarious. Dad gave a 'whoop' in all the wrong pauses and I was laughing so hard I had to go to the bathroom. Then I realised what a headache I had.

I groaned as I struggled to surface, for that was what it felt like: pushing up through thick black mire, and the weight of it all was on my head. When I opened my eyes it was dark, but I could tell I was lying face down into the back seat of a van. Every time it swerved, I dug my nails in to keep from rolling backwards. I lay still, for each time I moved, it felt as if the waves of nausea washing over the black mire would drown me, now that my head had finally emerged.

Lying half awake, I could hear the voices from the front seat. I could hardly understand a word, so they weren't speaking Urdu. I recognised the voice of the man who'd attacked me and I remembered the horror of the garden. I gingerly felt myself in the places I could reach, the most important ones anyway. As far as I could tell, it was only my head that had been attacked.

There was a deep chuckle from the driver's side of the vehicle. I was imagining things, of course, but it sounded as if the first voice had been apologising. Then he switched to Urdu.

'It was like she suspected foul play, Abu ji.'

'Perhaps she did not like you, my son.' More chuckles.

'She did not see me, nor did I expect her there so soon.'

The driver sounded older than the other, and he sighed. 'I, too, am sorry. I should have gone. That was the plan. Also she is no longer a child. I should have given more thought to the matter.'

'I had to hit her, you understand. She fought like a jackal.'

So it was a young guy who abducted me.

That was when I heard the older man's voice grow louder as though he'd turned to face the back. 'Whatever your fears, Sohail, there has been no mistake. I, myself, gave her that lapis hair clasp from my own shop.

'So,' and his voice was muffled again, coming from the front, 'when we arrive in Peshawar, we shall sound the alarm. We shall let those dogs know we have their precious little flower.'

Guess that was when they laughed some more and I didn't like it at all. Just then the horn blared as we passed a truck, the force of the wind making the little van shudder as it passed. But the sound that reduced me to tears was the van's horn. It played 'Für Elise', and it reminded me of home, of Mum and Dad, even of Uncle Jon, for his horn played 'Jingle Bells'. What would they do when they found out what had happened? *Oh Dad, if only you were here. You'd find me, I know you would. But I'm on my own, aren't I? No one knows.*

The horn blared again, further away this time. My head was hurting so badly, only sleep would fix it, and I tried to drift off, thinking how horns like that would be against the law in Australia. So much that was against the law in Australia happened every day in Pakistan.

When I came to again, there was no way I could hang on to what was threatening to heave out of my stomach. I dragged myself to the window, fumbled with the handle for an agonising few seconds and hung my head out, just in time. I was still thinking of Dad. He used to hate it when we chucked on the mountain roads, especially after he'd washed our van. At that moment a slight sob escaped out of my mouth—just enough noise for one of the men in the front to turn and jabber something to the other.

Immediately the van stopped and the younger man, Sohail, had the side door sliding open before both his feet touched the road. I was allowed out, thankful that I had the shawl to pull around my body to hide not only me, but also my fear and embarrassment. I breathed in the cool night air and felt the nauseous waves receding. Then I realised I didn't have anything to wipe my face with. I could still taste the vile remains of dinner and I knew, if I got back in the van like that, it wouldn't be long before I was sick again.

I was too scared to look up at him, so I mumbled in Urdu, 'Koi rumal hai? Do you have a handkerchief?' I imagined he would be staring at my shawl (Sonya's actually) as that's what a tribal girl would use to wipe her face.

'Rumal?' I asked again, determined to get a response, and suddenly he plunged his hand into his woollen vest pocket to pull out a handkerchief. He went off with it, just as I reached out my hand and I guessed he'd gone to wet the thing. For one mad instant I thought about running, but my head hurt so much I knew I wouldn't get far. Besides, I remembered how far he could jump. Strangely I didn't feel that evil presence any more—he was a known entity now. It may have been dangerous thinking, but a guy who goes to wet a handkerchief for you couldn't be totally bad. I didn't even wonder how he managed to have such a thing, just hoped it wouldn't be a bug-infested drain that he dipped it in.

Just as quickly as he'd disappeared, he was back. When he handed the handkerchief over, I noticed that his hand was the same colour as Dad's. He wasn't Pakistani, I knew that already. Afghan maybe? I ventured a glance upwards and, in the light from inside the van, I found him regarding me with equal interest. He swiftly averted his gaze as respectful Muslim men should, so I don't know why I was annoyed.

The engine revved up as the driver wrestled with the radio, drawing out sounds of the test series cricket. I climbed back in, keeping the handkerchief in case I needed it later. I refused the water one of them offered, as I knew it wouldn't be filtered, and I lay down, trying not to give in to the incredible wave of depression the sound of the cricket brought. They were playing in Australia; Dad and Andrew were supposed to be there.

Later I was awoken by the side door banging open again. One of the men was speaking to me, but as usual, I couldn't understand much. I could tell they wanted me out, though. I tottered to my feet and clung to the van door as the younger one addressed the driver as his father.

The tall, burly driver began to argue about something. 'Sohail—' but I lost concentration as I started to slip down the side of the van. There was an exclamation and the one called Sohail lifted me in his arms. I couldn't even struggle. My head was spinning as though I were travelling through a black tunnel on a roller coaster.

The cooler air outside helped a bit. It was dark and I could make out the night sounds of a bazaar. A horse clip-clopped by, pulling a tonga carriage, the animal snorting in anticipation of its rest and grain. I was carried down an unlit alleyway, into a building, up stairs that curved round and round so that I thought I was going to puke again, until we arrived on a flat roof above the bazaar. But the cool of the night air was short-lived. I was taken in through a door leading off the roof, a heavy piece of material dragging on my head as we went through.

Carpets again. I wrinkled my nose as the familiar smell met me at the doorway. Then the light was switched on and I was reminded of a rug shop that Dad had taken me to when I was younger. He had bought a prize carpet for Mum with flowers and borders, reds and blues. She always kept it by her bed. The smell of the wool and the second-hand carpets, which was a part of every Afghan rug shop, had permeated that shop as it did this one. Here, even the mud walls smelt of freshly sheared wool and sweaty second-hand tribal clothes that rug dealers display as antiques for unsuspecting tourists.

I was laid down, gently for a kidnapper, and I rested my head on a stuffed donkey bag, willing the dizziness to stop. Soon I heard the sound of teacups rattling and the guy called Sohail brought a little blue enamel teapot and an Afghan handle-less teacup for me to drink green tea.

That tea tasted so good. 'Shukriya, thank you,' I said in

Urdu, then sighed. The warm, sweet liquid stilled the waves in my stomach and with it, came strength and a little courage. I glanced up, trying not to look into those eyes that I knew would be waiting. But I didn't try hard enough and it was as I had thought: his eyes were green, but he was younger than I expected—no beard.

He was studying me strangely, differently from when we were by the van on the road. He said something, but I didn't understand him. Urdu was the only other language I learnt at school and I looked down at the teacup, trying not to let that prickling feeling behind my eyes develop into a flood. The way he was watching me was unnerving and as surely as one knows one will fall when a rope breaks, I knew there was more disaster impending.

Then I caught on to what he said as he spoke in Urdu.

'Are you understanding me now?'

I nodded miserably. 'Ji.' I sensed it wasn't what he wanted to hear.

With a violent movement that reminded me of the way Jasper was now, he stormed outside. I could hear male voices raised in anger and I shrank back into a corner. There were carpets everywhere: on the floor, on the walls, stacked in piles. Maybe if I could reach one and pull it over me, they wouldn't notice me. I felt like a huge blot on a page and I had the horrible impression the page would get torn out so the story could start again.

As suddenly as it began, the arguing stopped. I pulled the red shawl closer about me as the older man entered the room. He wore a huge wrapped turban and had an air of authority. No one would believe any of this back home. I don't know how things like this happen in Pakistan. As Dad used to say, that's the risk people take going to third-world countries close to war zones. He used to say things like that with a glint in his eye that gave me the impression he enjoyed dangerous spots. War zone? I was supposed to be having a holiday, visiting friends.

I watched the man slip off his shoes and come closer. I put down the cup and shrank further against the wall. He crouched on his haunches and peered at my downcast face for what seemed like ages, before letting out an angry burst of words.

My eyes were shut tight; I thought he'd strike me and I didn't think my head would take it, not again. When the blow didn't come I sneaked a look at him. He was just sitting there, wiping his eyes with his hand. He must have felt my attention on him as he looked up and spoke in Urdu.

'Beti, who are you? Do not fear. I will not hurt you.'

For an instant I hesitated; then, though I knew it was naïve, I believed him.

'I am the daughter of Wayne Richards,' I began in the way a girl would introduce herself in Pakistan, if there was no male to do it. 'I was staying at the house of Sonya Shklovsky …' I licked my lips wondering how much to say, 'when I was abducted.' It was a small moment of defiance; a Tom Thumb cracker going off when everyone else was watching rockets. I couldn't read his face to see if I'd angered him but I swallowed and continued while he was digesting what I'd said.

'Can you let me go? You could leave me here in Peshawar.' I'd guessed by then where we were. 'I have an uncle here, Jon Harris. He could come …' This plea achieved nothing, except to make me more upset.

'We will not hurt you,' the man repeated. I looked at his huge frame, his dark curly beard with streaks of grey, his turban, the empty cartridge holder crossing his chest, and I wondered if I was right to trust him. All he needed was a gun to look like one of those militants on the front page of the *Khyber Pakhtunkhwa Post*.

'Are you Americani?'

'Australivi.'

'That may be easier, at least.' He scratched his beard thoughtfully for a full minute, then he walked outside without a backward glance. So far, so good; maybe he'd let me go. I stood up, ready. But then I heard the click of a key turning in the door and my slightly raised spirits took another dive. No one was in any hurry to take me anywhere as I could hear the static roar of a crowd and the cultured excitement of a Pakistani commentator: 'It's out! No! The players are appealing. Smith is pleading with the umpire.'

'What a beautiful diving catch to his right …' I pricked up my ears at the Australian accent but the Pakistani voice cut in, 'The umpire is shaking his head. Not out! Younis Khan is not out!' And the crowd roared again.

I settled down on the rough donkey bag to wait. Something would have to happen sooner or later, and I understood enough about cricket fanatics to know it wouldn't be until the day's play was over.

9

Jasper

Jasper slammed the Suzuki door shut. It was the first time he'd driven so far at night, and he found his hands were shaking when he finally turned the engine off. Driving in Pakistan was nothing like in the West. Trucks, always top-heavy and travelling too fast on the wrong side of the road, commanded the night roads to escape the day traffic. Huge, gaudy, overcrowded buses were driven crazily as if the drivers believed invisible tracks (they called it fate) would keep them from crashing over the edge. It was amazing how people, who seemed calm and patient, could transform into The Joker as soon as they sat behind a steering wheel.

Liana put a hand on his. 'You did well, Jasper, and I wouldn't have thought you'd have had much driving experience.'

'I haven't. Dad used to let me drive when …' He stopped and abruptly faced the other way. Liana spoke softly to his back. 'You okay?' She sounded gentle and offhand at the same time. He knew that tone girls got when they felt he needed to 'offload' but he didn't need their help, nor Liana's.

'Sure.' He turned back towards her, hoping anger didn't

show in his eyes, in case she thought it was directed at her. This was where he grew up. It was the first time he'd been back since his father disappeared, and there he was, pretending to grin at her so she'd think everything was all right.

Sonya seemed involved in thoughts of her own and turned around a few times. 'We should go down this gali, I think.' And she pointed down a dark narrow alleyway. It didn't take much to wipe the grin off Jasper's face.

'You think? Hell, Sonya. Peshawar is not a place where I like to be out in the middle of the night! Either you know where to go or you don't. Got it?'

Sonya faced him, her chin even higher than usual. 'That way, then.' And she pointed down the same alley. Whatever Jasper thought of Sonya, she at least was strong willed. Jasper waited, tapping his foot on a discarded cigarette box while the girls adjusted their shawls to cover their faces. They then made their way after him, as custom dictated, down the narrow alley. Shouting started up not far away and a machine gun fired, making Liana pause.

'It may be just a wedding,' Jasper said, offering reassurance that he didn't feel. 'A few years ago, we were at a wedding here where the guests got so trigger-happy they had a contest to see who could fire closest to the bridal couple without hitting them. They wounded the groom and killed the bride—by accident—and they were just having fun!'

'After a story like that, I'm not meant to worry?' Liana said.

The truth was Jasper knew Peshawar could be a dangerous place. So many of the refugees lived there, and among them, the Taliban militants, many of whom would take on the world to keep their country holy and would gladly die doing so. They were told they'd go straight to Paradise if killed in a holy cause, and many were such extreme hotheads that fervour spread through a mob of them like a summer brushfire.

It was Sonya who worried Jasper more. She showed none of the nervousness that she should feel, and when they heard that chilling sound—the click of a safety catch being released—from the alley on their left, Sonya hardly moved a muscle. Jasper jumped, so did Liana as she was close beside him, and he felt the tremor right through his leather jacket.

Jasper's hissed, 'Don't panic', was superfluous. Sonya ignored him and Liana froze at the size of the gun the Pakhtun was holding. She looked on the verge of panic but one glance at Jasper's face seemed to calm her; he tried to put on an act of bravado.

'Raza! Come!' The man motioned them down the alley he had emerged from. Jasper was surprised; the guy didn't seem much older than himself. Then he mentally chided himself. How could he be thinking about how old the guy was when their lives could be on the line? It was as though his mind had switched off.

'Jasper?' Liana found his arm and hung on. She seemed relieved he didn't pull away. 'How will we find Jaime, now?'

He only shook his head. Then, for the first time that night, he was actually pleased. 'I know where we are. We're behind the Kissah Kahani—the street of the storytellers. It's the oldest part of the bazaar.'

Liana wasn't impressed. 'It's like a rabbit warren. We could never find our way out of this again.'

'I could,' came Jasper's stubborn whisper.

10

Jaime

When I first heard the clunk of the lock, I thought it would be the older Afghan man coming back to ask more questions. I sat up straighter because I'd been thinking of offering my gold bangle as payment, if they'd let me go. The light went on and I shut my eyes momentarily against the glare.

'Jaime! Is that you?'

My eyelids flew open. It sounded just like Liana at the airport. And suddenly she was hugging me. They were all there, Sonya and Jasper too. They'd been pushed in and the door locked behind them. Sonya's face looked like a lake on a calm day, nothing remarkable you could say about it, except it was pretty, but Jasper was a dam about to burst.

'Are you all right?' Liana was feeling my bones.

I nodded. 'My head feels bad, but it's better since I've been asleep.'

Jasper crouched beside me. 'Jaime, are you really okay?' I looked up at him. I knew what he meant and I nodded again. His eyes grew bright, and he quickly looked away.

Liana was beside herself. She was big on miracles and

was going on about how special it was to find me when they had no idea where I was. But the more she said, the bigger Jasper's scowl grew until finally he cut in.

'You're forgetting something, Li. She,' and he pointed at Sonya, 'knew where Jaime was. She led us into a trap.' He walked—stalked was more like it—over to Sonya, so he could talk right into her face.

'I think we have you to thank for this mess. Would you care to do some explaining?'

Even Sonya seemed to see that Jasper couldn't be pushed any more. She answered him straight away. 'I was the one they wanted. Jaime should not have been taken.'

I still didn't see what she meant, but Jasper seemed to. 'You little bitch. You set her up, didn't you? Look at her. She's the same height, same colour hair, the same shawl you wore the other night.' And the clip, I silently added. Could he be right? Half of me was shocked. I'd never heard him quite so worked up, and I wanted to soothe him, say it would be okay, but I wanted to hear what he thought about it more.

Sonya's eyes shone so gold they sparked. 'You forget! I warned the girls. I told them not to go into the garden.'

'There wasn't a prowler, was there?'

'No.' Sonya's tone was quiet but short.

I had a question too. 'So how did you know something was going to happen in the garden?'

There was no answer at first, then she sighed. 'I had a text.' She always gave me the impression she didn't think I was worth talking to.

'And then you told your friend in the carpet shop?' Jasper

accused. 'Is that what you were doing last night?' Sonya shut her lips together as tight as Ali Baba's cave. Perhaps Jasper realised she had said all she intended to, or maybe her quietness proved something to him, as he gave up questioning her, and began to make himself comfortable on the floor with a few of the carpets and woven rugs.

Liana voiced the question that was crowding my mind. 'What happens now?'

'One thing's for sure.' Jasper was smoothing a Kashmiri shawl over the carpets so they wouldn't itch him in the night. 'Those Pakhtuns want Sonya for some reason. But what about the rest of us? We just got in the way. Guys like that, who kidnap people, are not about to let us go so we can tell the whole world about it.'

I felt I needed to put him right; Jasper didn't have all the facts. 'They said they wouldn't hurt me.'

'What crap!'

'Jasper, do you mind?'

'Look at you. You have a king-sized bruise across your forehead and you can't even sit up straight. The worst state I've ever seen you in. And Junior out there …' He paused momentarily as if he couldn't find words to say that wouldn't self-destruct on utterance. He settled on the gun instead. 'That AK 47 he's carrying around is the meanest assault rifle I've ever seen close up. Do you know what size hole that would make in these walls if it went off?'

'Anyway, since they've taken our phones and there's no getting out of here tonight, I'm going to sleep. Can't think why they've left me in here with you girls.' He was looking at me as he added, 'Must think you're my sisters.'

I soon found myself wondering if he were right. I needed to feel there was a way out, but Jasper had taken that fragile security away, making it seem as though there wasn't any hope. I fell asleep imagining the walls would close in on us while we dreamed our lives away.

اله

The winter morning light stretched yellow fingers across my donkey bag, forcing one of my eyes open and then the other. Jasper was already awake, examining rugs in a corner of the shop. He glanced up as I stirred.

'Glad to see you've joined the land of the living.'

'You could call it that.'

'These carpets are well made. Come and see.' As I crawled to where he was kneeling, he turned one of the carpets over. 'See, double-knotted too.'

'You know much about carpets, Jas?'

'Maybe too little not to get ripped off, but enough to enjoy them.'

'Whenever Dad bought a carpet, it was like a full-scale campaign. It took days. Once he was treated to a feast. He bought that man's carpet. I don't think there was any way he could get out of it. He gave it to Mum; she loved the flowers on it. It had the same design as this one, but the border on this is slightly different. I thought each particular design was supposed to be identical.'

'Only Allah can make something perfect,' Jasper said and I grinned, relieved he was in a better mood than the night before. 'You'll find a mistake in every one of them, put there purposely so He won't get angry.'

'This whole border pattern is different though. It can't be just a mistake.'

'They are made here—in Peshawar.' Sonya's voice sounded muffled as though she was in the middle of a yawn.

'Here?' Liana echoed. 'But a true Turkmen carpet should be made in Afghanistan, surely?'

'A true one, yes. But that is a copy. Once they were made by refugees in the camps, now by Pakistani workers here. If the carpet dealer is honest, he will tell the customer and charge less.'

'And if he's not honest?' Liana queried.

Sonya shrugged her shoulders.

We heard the sound of brass in the lock and there was Sohail silhouetted in the doorway, a tray balanced on one hand. Some moments stand out more in the memory. That was one of them for me. It was as though we were all part of a frozen tableau and I could see all the others' faces at once. Liana's mouth was open. She looked like I must have when I saw Suneel, a Chitrali guy, before we left Pakistan a year ago. I think it's the thought of the unobtainable that makes some guys from different cultures so attractive. Sohail seemed more Liana's age too.

Sonya, strangely enough, took one quick look upward and promptly stared at the floor, all before he would have had any eye contact with her. She didn't look scared, yet demure was the last word I would have used to describe her. Her behaviour mystified me.

Jasper, beside me, looked as if murder was about to be committed. I hoped he could control himself long enough for us to eat breakfast. I was hungry.

Sohail set the tray down without saying a word and

glanced around the room before departing. I watched him duck his red-capped head under the carpet hanging above the door as he went, and I knew, without checking, that Liana had watched him too.

'Breakfast,' she murmured, as if from far away.

'At least he left the door open this time,' I prattled on, trying to bring some normality into the room again.

Liana set out the little teacups that looked like miniature Chinese bowls. 'Hey, there's jam in the eggs!'

'Gross! I don't think I could face that.' I giggled, which earned me an annoyed glance from Jasper. I wished he'd lighten up. We weren't being ill-treated; jam in scrambled eggs was a dish served to guests in Afghan households and he should have known that. 'Could I have a piece of naan please, Li?'

She passed the flat bread across with a cup full of milky sweet tea. Jasper and I were closest to the door, but it was a while before I noticed that he wasn't concentrating on his food.

'Jasper?'

He put a finger before his mouth. 'I'm listening.'

I glanced at the others. Liana was having a one-sided conversation with Sonya. That won't last long, I was thinking when I realised that Jasper's ear was cocked to the roof outside. There were more than two men out there and the discussion didn't seem to be about the cricket.

'What're they saying?' I hoped Jasper wouldn't shush me again.

'It's in the papers this morning.'

'About us?'

He nodded without looking at me. 'Even the English one. We were followed from Islamabad.'

'Who by?'

He didn't answer.

'They're saying they have to go now, it's not safe.'

'Why? Who for?'

'They're saying you and Sonya look alike.'

'What's that got to do with it?'

Jasper lifted a hand for quiet. The older man began talking. I bent closer to ask Jasper what the man said, when he clutched my hand. I was so surprised, I couldn't say anything. Then I saw that Jasper's mouth was open. The hand holding mine clenched even tighter.

'Jasper!' He was hurting me. 'What's wrong?'

'I've heard that voice before.'

'Whose?' He was so exasperating, and then he was staring at Sonya. I followed his gaze and even I was mesmerised. She was busy dunking naan in her tea. I'd only seen Afghans do that.

'How on earth did she learn to do that?'

A shadow fell across us then, and we looked up at the doorway.

'Assalamu Alaikum, peace be to you,' greeted the older Pakhtun standing there, smiling at us all.

'Wa Alaikum Assalam,' Jasper answered, even though he scowled. In captivity, the rules of hospitality were still observed, it seemed.

The man crouched onto his haunches in the centre of the room and poured himself a cup of tea. 'It seems to me that we must make a journey,' he said in Urdu after his first mouthful. 'I want you to understand that this is for your own safety.' He wiped his beard with his hand and looked directly at Jasper. It was interesting how in Pakistan the most important decisions were made between the men, or was it only out of respect for our feminine persons that he didn't look directly at any of us girls? I thought Sonya would have protested but she sat looking at the floor, as demure as any Pakistani girl. I couldn't make her out. She seemed to have undergone a character transplant.

'I also want you to understand that there will be no thoughts of escape.' He sounded like Dad warning my brother Andrew about 'monkey business' on a picnic. 'If I am to look after you, I must have your full cooperation. Do you understand?'

We girls nodded. Jasper sat stunned as though he'd been hit over the head with a mallet and hadn't started slipping down the wall yet. The man pulled up his great frame. 'We leave in fifteen minutes.' Then he smiled. It was very confusing for he didn't seem evil at all.

'You may call me "Uncle" when you refer to me.' He looked pleased with his own benign gesture. 'Ma yarega warra!' Strangely he seemed to be looking in Sonya's direction when he said that though it was in Pakhtu. I was about to ask Jasper what it meant when the man translated it into Urdu himself. 'Do not be frightened, children.'

Jasper was staring at him walking out through the doorway.

'Are you all right, Jas?' He didn't answer straight away and when he did, it changed everything.

'I remember where I heard that voice.' He glanced over at Sonya again.

'Where?'

'It's the voice I heard with Sonya. In the carpet shop.'

'He was there?' I shifted so I could see out the door too. Sohail had just handed a Kalashnikov to 'Uncle' to hold and, as he turned and smiled at his son, it was then that Jasper stiffened.

'I've seen him too. He's the one!'

'Who, Jas?'

'He's the Pakhtun posing with my dad in the photograph I saw in the carpet shop.'

11

Jaime

The next day I was beginning to feel more like my old self again—the way I used to be when we lived in Pakistan. The last year in Australia had made me feel like a cushion with the stuffing knocked out of it. By the end of the year, I had finally begun feeling as if I belonged there, but I still had a long road to travel.

Now that I was back in Pakistan, even though I'd never expected my holiday to turn out like this, it was still my known world. It was weird, but I was thinking that morning, as the Pakhtuns bundled us into a faded blue Ford van, us girls clad in blue burqas to match, that I'd rather die here where things were familiar and I understood the cultural cues.

Liana didn't seem so sure; she looked like she'd had a premonition of disaster. Though, whatever she may have been feeling, I believed she was stronger than she used to be years ago and I gave her a nudge to dispel her thoughts.

'Can you imagine what Ayesha would say if she could see us in these Afghan burqas?' I knew I must have looked like a blue shuttlecock, clad from top to toe in pleated cotton.

'Poor Ayesha,' Li said. 'She tries to be more Western than we are, even though she's Pakistani.'

'Maybe it's the lure of something different.' I lifted up the hem of the burqa and breathed in deeply as I leaned forward to stare out the window of the moving van. Even though it was winter, the heavy material made me feel as though my air supply was squeezed off, and I wiped the sweat from my upper lip.

Swiftly, Sohail loomed towards me from his seat opposite. I'd forgotten about him momentarily. 'Put the veil down!' he hissed in Urdu. 'Immediately!'

Startled, I did as he said, and slowly settled back into my seat next to Liana. I glanced across to Sonya but she seemed to be asleep. 'So much for that,' I murmured in a flat little voice and when I saw Sohail staring at me from across the van, I made a face at him behind the mesh of the veil. It was childish, but satisfying. I could see out but no one could see in. I chuckled when I realised there was a worthwhile use for burqas after all.

'I suppose they gave us these to wear so nobody would recognise us,' I suggested to Liana, trying to make conversation.

'Guess you're right.' She didn't sound annoyed exactly, just dry—I'd said the obvious and she didn't want to be reminded of it. That was enough to keep me quiet for a while. At least I could see through the window from where I sat. The bazaar was crowded and even in winter, Peshawar was a dusty, dirty place. Street vendors sold their wares, trying to outdo each other, shouting their prices and the merits of their products. Men sat in groups outside the teashops, listening to radios or watching TVs. The cricket, no doubt. Children, wrapped in torn shawls, playing by the side of the road, seemed unaware of the traffic and only moved aside in response to the sharp blast of a horn.

Suddenly, I stood up, clutching hold of Liana's shoulder. 'Hey! Isn't that Uncle Jon's jeep? Jasper, you know Jon Harris. Isn't that his car?' I was trying to get closer to the window, stumbling over the rolled carpets underfoot, when a hand shot out and pushed me down abruptly, and there was Sohail breathing into my burqa. I didn't dare move a muscle for I couldn't tell if he could see me that close.

'Have you gone mad? You fool! You could spoil everything!' I stared at him, speechless. What could I spoil? Their plan to abduct us? Wasn't that my job? Yet he made it sound as though I was putting everyone in danger.

I held my breath as Jasper moved towards Sohail. It was barely noticeable but, like a jungle cat, Sohail swung round, picked up the assault rifle, and sat back in his seat with the gun levelled at the other boy. Jasper's eyes, like mine, were on Sohail's finger as it rested on the gunlock. It all happened in a moment, and Jasper slowly leaned back. I breathed again. If looks alone could kill, Sohail would have been flapping like a landed fish on the floor, gasping for his last breath.

After a while, Sohail lowered the rifle and threw a command at the driver. The same cultured Pakistani accent from the night before gave judgements on cricket players' performance and stats. Younis Khan was heading for a century. I was beginning to realise that besides guns, Sohail's other passion in life was cricket. I turned to Liana.

'Pity the series wasn't playing here in Pakistan; we could have got a message back to Australia—through the cricket team. I could've sent my bangle with a note.' I wasn't serious, just trying to lighten everything up. It didn't work.

'I hope you're joking,' she said. 'Our handsome Pakhtun here wouldn't let you near the window, for a start. And, secondly, if anyone got their hands on that bangle, they'd pawn it in the bazaar. Most probably keep their whole family clothed and fed for a year. Anyway, it's the embassy that has to do something. Maybe the school has notified them by now.'

'Yeah.' And that was when I saw the Khyber Pass spread out before us. It was just like the photos in travel books: a huge road meandering between the mountains like a serpent. Dad had never been able to take me when we were living there. There was so much red tape and you had to hire an armed guard to protect you while you drove through to Afghanistan.

I was about to tell Jasper, when he saw it too. I noticed the muscle tighten in his cheek and wondered what was wrong. Then I remembered that it wouldn't be anything remarkable for him; he'd probably seen it before. It was Liana who sounded the alarm.

She turned to Sohail. 'You're taking us to Afghanistan!' I knew she was upset as she spoke in English.

'He can't understand you.' Jasper sounded weary and looked as if he were about to translate into Pakhtu when Sohail spoke.

'On the contrary, I am understanding.'

There was a silence. So many things had gone wrong that I hardly knew what to deal with first. I wanted to know how come he knew English. At that point, I wasn't fully aware of the other danger.

'How …?' I didn't get far.

'I attended school in Kabul. I studied English there.'

All of a sudden I felt annoyed and stupid. I tried

to remember how many times I'd used the wrong Urdu words to explain things when all the time he could have understood my English.

'Then why didn't you say so?'

'Your Urdu is better than my English,' he snapped. 'There was no need.' His voice faded in dismissal but I wasn't finished with him yet. I didn't believe my Urdu was better than his English and suddenly he seemed more vulnerable, more part of the things I could understand. I glanced across at Liana for moral support, and the strained way she was sitting made me remember her words about Afghanistan. I persisted.

'You are, aren't you? Taking us across the border. Isn't it dangerous? There's still fighting. Mines. No Westerners without permits are allowed near the Khyber Pass, let alone across the border. We'll never be found …' I realised what I'd said and shut my mouth.

Sohail smiled politely at me. He was obviously used to ladies in burqas. He treated me exactly as if there was nothing on my face at all.

'I see you are an intelligent girl. That is good.'

I turned towards Jasper, hoping he'd back me up. He must have known I was looking at him, but he ignored me. There was nothing he could do anyway; the gun was still trained his way. Sonya was quiet behind her veil. There was no way of working out what she thought of it all, nor did I feel like asking her. She had a habit of not hearing me when I spoke to her.

There was nothing else to do except look out the window. There was one good thing: I was finally getting to see the Hindu Kush up close. They were what I called 'forever' mountains; the type that must have existed from the beginning of creation and always would. I tried surreptitiously to lift my burqa so Sohail wouldn't notice. I needed more air. Then I inched a bit closer to Jasper. He looked so frustrated. He was brought up in a country where men protect those in their care. By then I was sure Jasper thought of Liana and me in that light and I felt sorry for him. He looked like Superman confronted with kryptonite and I wanted to tell him he didn't have to take such a load on himself.

'Jasper,' I whispered. 'Are you okay?'

This time he sort of grinned. 'Guess so.' I was relieved as I wasn't sure any more what reaction I'd get from him.

'You look so worried.'

'I am. I'd like to get some answers out of that great hulking Pakhtun. But he hasn't come. He got Junior to do the dirty work.'

'Do you think they'll let us go later?'

'I don't know. But I do know kidnappers are the lowest of the low. I've heard about what happens …' He stopped as though he'd said too much. I was glad. I didn't want to hear what he'd heard. For some strange reason, I didn't feel totally kidnapped. Maybe it was my mind helping me through, maybe it was my belief in a God who works things out for the best, or maybe I was just naïve. I stared out at those mountains and all I saw was their beauty. They weren't covered in pines like the ones near our school, but they were magnificent in their snowy starkness.

'They look cruel,' Liana murmured, following my gaze.

'Who?'

'The mountains.'

It made me think it was beliefs and attitudes that make people strong, and I hoped I could stay positive through whatever lay ahead. Liana again kicked back the carpet that had rolled out from under our seat. I helped her as the van swerved round another sharp bend. 'Why are they bringing carpets into Afghanistan anyway? I thought the market was in Pakistan.'

'I don't know, Jaime. Maybe for their own use. Yuck. I feel sick. This road is worse than the one up the mountain to the school.'

Talk about the power of suggestion. It wasn't long before I felt like chucking too. I tried to hold it down but soon had to lift my burqa and take a dive for the window, whether Sohail liked it or not. Surprisingly, the young Pakhtun motioned for the driver to stop, then swung out, rifle in one hand, as he pulled open the side door with the other. Both Liana and I tumbled out, pulling in shuddering breaths of cold mountain air. It seemed ages before the ground stilled and I could walk steadily again.

Jasper climbed out too and as he passed Sohail, he turned back to face the Pakhtun. 'Those burqas are stifling in the van. Can't they leave them off?'

'Not until we reach the safety of my home. It is not far, our village is on the next ridge.'

I looked up to find the view breathtaking and heart-rending all at the same time. Snow-topped mountains loomed ahead, and nestled in front was a village. Even from that distance I could see the dots that meant animals and shepherds, but I could also see that all was not well with the village and the land about it. Dad said Afghanistan was once called the Land of Orchards, but now there was hardly a tree in sight. Entire fields around the village were uncultivated and in some places, where I presumed houses should have been, there was just rubble.

I walked closer to the edge of the road and Sohail followed me. I looked back and saw Jasper watching us. It was easy to imagine what he was thinking—suspicion was written all over his face. Sonya stepped out of the van then. She was weird, didn't seem worried at all; just looked around as though she was on a Sunday afternoon drive.

Sohail was close enough now for me to be aware of him standing there and I wasn't sure whether to ignore him or not. I'd thrown back the burqa and the cold wind was making my nose run, so I rummaged in my pockets for a tissue. Sohail shifted the Kalashnikov to his shoulder but paused when I drew out his newly washed handkerchief. I knew he was staring at me; I could feel the weight of his gaze resting on my head. I glanced up and gaped. He was smiling at me!

'You seem to make a habit of being ill, little sister.' The shock of his addressing me like that after all the fuss in the van made my annoyance disappear. I was sure he wasn't supposed to talk to me so personally. Maybe I should have walked away but I took another look at him instead. He didn't seem mean at all with that smile on his face; it reached right up to his green eyes. I bent my head, ashamed of myself. What was I doing? The smile was most probably more dangerous than his gun.

In an effort to act normal I blew my nose, then remembered it was bad manners to blow your nose in front of an Afghan. Couldn't I do anything right? I sneaked another look at him and I could see the scar where I'd ripped his cheek that other night. He was gazing up at the village. He didn't look offended, just proud and noble. Shareef, Pakistanis would say. Then I felt stupid as I imagined Jasper's disgust if he could read my thoughts.

Liana came over and addressed Sohail. 'There was fighting in your village?' I was thankful for the diversion.

He turned back to regard us both. 'There has always been fighting and still is. Now some people are returning. From Pakistan, Iran. We are rebuilding. Planting new trees.' He saw me staring at a field beyond him where a man was leading a pair of oxen around, pulling a plough. 'The people from my village have always tried to sow their crops, even during the fighting. But with no rain, they starve.' There was nothing I could say.

Liana had been scrutinising the mountains behind us. 'There's a fort up there.' She pointed it out as I shaded my eyes, following her gaze. There was a long stone wall snaking along the high rocky ridge. A shelled-out tank sat halfway up, looking like a trophy on a mantelshelf. 'The fort looks hundreds of years old. It would be fun to explore it.'

Sohail's amiable expression switched off as quickly as electricity in a Pakistani power failure. 'You will never go there. It is a dangerous place.'

'Why?' I plucked up the courage to ask, even though he looked like the old Sohail in the van.

'The people there are terrorists. They lose their tempers over the least thing and shoot at anything that moves for no reason at all.' And suddenly, as if to prove his point, he threw up the machine gun and with both hands, let off a round of ammunition into the air. The sound ricocheted off the rocky mountain wall and reverberated round the valley. No one spoke as the sound died away. Even Sonya looked startled.

My hands were on my ears. The noise had been deafening

and the fifteen seconds or so that it had taken to empty the magazine seemed like minutes. They were terrorists? What about him? I didn't want to meet anyone with a bigger gun or more passion than he had. I glanced over at Jasper and realised with a jolt that he'd been ready to move towards us, and in that brief instant, I thought I'd caught something else in his expression: the urge to protect a girl he cared for.

The moment passed and Sohail strode over to the van, motioning us all to follow.

'He's crazy,' Jasper muttered as I got within earshot. 'That's all we need—a crazy guy with an AK 47.'

Sohail directed us all into the van as if a horde of terrorists were swarming down the hill. There weren't any—I checked. As we girls were climbing in, Sohail said in a softer tone to us, 'You must veil yourselves with the burqas for your safety. Please, until we arrive at my home.'

I was thinking about that 'please' for quite a while afterwards. Who had ever heard of an abductor saying please?

12

Jaime

Sohail's house was nothing like I'd imagined. I was expecting a small village home, rough and dark like the carpet shop in Peshawar; yet there, in the heart of a remote mountain village, was a rambling whitewashed mud-brick house. It was tin-roofed with a spacious courtyard decorated with potted plants, all surrounded by the usual four-metre wall. It was remarkably well preserved, considering the amount of time war had raged in the country.

I was still eyeing the height of the wall when servants appeared from all directions to take the carpets and other luggage (which seemed to consist of bags of wheat and food, plus long canvas-covered bundles). Children wrapped in blankets stood around, shyly curious. One was on crutches; he had only one leg. I smiled at them, presuming they'd be servants' kids. One returned me a sticky grin, his hand clutching a sucked orange.

Soon we were being shown into a room with exquisite Turkmen rugs scattered on the floor as if it were the most normal thing in the world to have such treasure walked on. I recognised some of the patterns that Dad used to drool over in carpet shops, saying they weren't for the likes of us.

Sohail motioned for us to sit on carpet cushions while sweet green tea was brought. I used the time to take off the heavy burqa.

'I'm sure glad to get out of this at last,' I murmured to Liana, but she didn't answer. She seemed too engrossed in what was happening, as Sohail suddenly stood in delight to greet a middle-aged, plump lady who had hurried into the room. She clasped both his hands and turned her smooth cheeks from side to side so he could kiss her. After the greeting, Sohail let his eyes sweep from her dark hair down to her tiny gold-slippered feet; then he poured out a torrent of Pakhtu.

The look of pleasure on her face faded slightly as she looked in surprise at us, but then she gave such an infectious smile that I had to smile back. Even Sonya did, I noticed. Only Jasper seemed unmoved by the lady's beauty and charm. I was close enough to him to risk a quick whisper.

'Don't you think she's nice?'

The look he turned on me frightened me as much as Sohail had in the van. 'We haven't just dropped in for chai. We're kidnapped. In Afghanistan! A conflict zone. Doesn't anybody remember?' He looked past me at Liana, who seemed totally enthralled by the picture of Sohail and the woman. The force of Jasper's whisper shocked me; the anger and sarcasm hurt too. It made me want to justify myself.

'But, Jas, we haven't been hurt ...'

His whisper shot back fast. 'If you can be taken in so easily, how can we ever hope to get out of here? Wake up, Jaime. We're not in fairyland. These people can be dangerous—the Taliban haven't disappeared. This village might be working with them.'

I turned to study Sohail and the lady who must have been his mother. She didn't look like a terrorist, though it did seem Sohail was persuading her about something.

Sohail finally faced us all. 'My mother only speaks Pakhtu and Persian. But my cousin, Nazira, is here and will help you in any way. Nazira!'

A girl appeared in the doorway. She wasn't much older than me and she didn't look as if she wanted to help in any way whatsoever. 'How do you do?' she finally said in grammar-book-English after much nonverbal prompting from her cousin.

'Fine, thank you,' I answered. I caught Jasper's exasperated look to the ceiling.

'She is making an effort,' I hissed to him. He was so annoying. Nazira wasn't any part of this; why take it out on her? He gestured towards Sonya and I was just in time to see a sharp look cast in Nazira's direction. It was the most emotion I'd seen Sonya show all day.

'She's another problem,' Jasper said.

'Who? Sonya?'

'At least she's never boring.'

I stared at him with nothing to say. What on earth did he mean? He had certainly become more complicated than I remembered him to be when we were kids.

There wasn't time to query him, as we girls were taken to a room where we would sleep at night. It too was covered in rugs and beautiful hand-woven wall hangings. Nazira also slept there and on occasions so would Mrs Kumar, Sohail's mother. Nazira had just finished telling us that Sohail's father was often referred to as a war lord or commander. So that was why Sohail's father had that commanding presence. War lords never received good press in Western media and I tried not to show that she had frightened me.

She looked both proud and belligerent whenever she spoke to us, and I was sure she was even ruder to Sonya than to Liana or me. She always served Sonya last if she brought food and never asked her if she needed anything like she unwillingly did to Liana and me. I thought at the time it was because Sonya was Russian. Besides, Sonya wasn't too friendly either, so what could one expect?

Later that first day, we girls sat on the floor, eating Kabuli pilau, rice with chunks of mutton, sweet carrot pieces and cooked raisins in it. Over the top had been sprinkled roasted almonds.

'Excellent food.' I raised my eyebrows at Liana for a response.

'Sure is, but don't get your sleeve in it.'

'That's another thing.' I changed my position on the rug. 'Can you believe Mrs Kumar gave us these outfits?' I fingered the intricate embroidery on the bodice and smoothed out the gathers in the front. 'The colours are so rich. I've always wanted a tribal Afghan dress like this.' I got up and twirled around the others in a red and green cloud, the matching pants, gathered at the ankle, billowing out as I turned.

Liana watched me, peaceful for once with a contented smile on her face. 'You're right, you know. Mrs Kumar treats us like long-lost relatives come home.'

Sonya suddenly spluttered and dropped her spoon as she coughed.

'You okay, Sonya?' I stopped prancing. 'Here, have some water.' I leaned down to the tray and handed Sonya a glass.

'I am all right.' She took a sip. 'Some rice went the wrong way.' She even gave one of her rare smiles. With her coughing fit subsided, Sonya surveyed us with more interest than she'd done since that first day at the American school.

'You like it here, do you not?' she finally asked.

'Sure,' I answered. 'Mrs Kumar is great, and even Sohail seems kinder now as if he's apologising for what's happened.'

Sonya raised her eyebrows as if she thought that was a childish revelation, but didn't comment.

'You know what?' Liana said. 'I don't think Mrs Kumar knows we're abducted. Do you, Sonya?'

Sonya hesitated, then sighed almost wearily. 'No, I do not think she knows. I believe she thinks that you are my friends and Jasper is your brother.'

'She thinks we're sisters?' I thought of Liana's hair and skin so much darker than mine.

'Why not? You have the same accent and Liana is three years older than you, is she not?'

I nodded.

'I don't understand.' Liana's forehead screwed up, causing little furrow marks between her eyes. 'What do you mean "friends of yours"? Does she know you?'

'No, she does not—but she was expecting me one day.' Then Sonya's voice became softer so that I had to lean closer. 'Although not at this time.'

I was itching to ask what she meant but just then Nazira

padded in with green tea on a tray, and Sonya shook her head slightly, warning us not to say anything else.

We didn't get another chance to speak to Sonya alone that day. I was glad they thought Jasper was our brother because it meant he was allowed to visit.

The next afternoon he was let in and we were left alone, as it was considered 'unseemly' for Sonya or Nazira to be in the same room with him since he wasn't their relative and was old enough to be married. I grinned to myself thinking of Jasper in that light, but in those villages the people marry young: boys seventeen and girls only fourteen.

I shuddered, imagining what might happen if they found out he was American, and not our brother. Even if they didn't hurt him, our link with the outside would be gone, as well as the emotional support that—believe it or not—he managed to give. Still, Sonya was the only one who knew and she didn't seem to think the secret worth telling.

Jasper also had on Afghan tribal clothes: the baggy trousers, a long shirt and a sheepskin vest, called a poshteen, with the fleece worn on the inside. When I first saw him like that and with a hand-embroidered colourful cap set back on his dark head, I couldn't believe it was him—he could have passed as Sohail's brother. I didn't dare say so; that would have ruined the whole visit.

'You both look fine,' he said as he sat on the floor. 'Are you really? No one hassling you or anything?'

We both shook our heads and I couldn't help thinking that whatever changes of mood he tended to go through, he did genuinely care for us.

'They let me go to the bazaar if I wear these clothes.' He

smiled ruefully, probably knowing it was because he was a guy. 'I'm sorry you can't go out.'

'We have a courtyard.' I tried to sound enthusiastic as I didn't want him getting morose and angry again. 'The sun comes in and it's pretty. The walls are high though.'

'Don't worry about us, Jas,' Liana said gently. 'We're being well treated, just like family.'

'That's what I can't work out,' Jasper said. 'Nothing is ever what it seems here. They say one thing but mean another.' He stood up abruptly and paced the room. I watched him with a sinking feeling in my middle. The calm had been short-lived.

'Here we are—hostages! Everyone smiles, kills the fatted calf and gives us new clothes. Mrs Kumar—'

'She doesn't know,' I interrupted, diving for the handkerchief. A sneeze was coming on.

'No, I didn't think so, but all the same, there's something sinister going on. When people smile and carry on normally, it's worse than if they point a gun at you. At least then you know where you—' He stopped suddenly and I looked up. He was staring at me wiping my nose. I couldn't believe what he did next. He strode over and snatched the handkerchief right out of my hands.

'Hey, Jas. There's no need to be so dramatic.'

He didn't even hear me. 'Where did you get this?' was all he said, his voice sounding so tightly stretched it might break.

'From Sohail. I keep meaning to give it back. Why?'

Jasper ignored the question and spread the handkerchief out on a cushion. In one corner were embroidered the initials, 'J P'.

'I didn't notice that.' My voice came out slightly strangled. Liana traced the letters with her finger.

'J P … Jasper Pembley. Is it yours?' Her brow furrowed.

The spring finally stretched too tight and I heard the crack in his voice. 'I remember when Mum was stitching this. I was eleven years old. I was home from school for the weekend at Peshawar. The next day was Father's Day and I wanted something special to give him.

'"J P" is for Joe Pembley—my father!'

13

Jaime

There was nothing Jasper could do about his father's handkerchief except keep it to remind him of his dad. Those early days turned into a week, then two, three weeks, until I began to feel we'd always been in Mrs Kumar's house. Sonya seemed to relax, although she still had that tensed attitude of a cat ready to spring at the first sign of trouble. At times I'd find her pacing the floor in our room or sitting in a pensive mood, staring out the window into the courtyard.

Once I climbed the wall and saw the fields beyond the mosque. It looked like whole families at work, ploughing with an implement that I later found had been made from the shell of an old armoured tank. There were fat-tailed sheep, donkeys and a horse grazing, a few men digging holes probably to plant trees when winter finished. I wondered if we could get away, but it seemed too dangerous. There were mines, for a start. Every so often we would hear the dull boom and feel the floor shudder as another one exploded. A few men in the village had been trained by someone like Uncle Jon to clear the area of mines. Sonya said there were over ten million mines in the country and at the speed of those men who were de-activating the Kumars' village, it'd take four thousand years to clear all of Afghanistan. I had no idea how she knew all that stuff or even how she managed to sound genuinely concerned about it.

One thing was for sure—Mrs Kumar wasn't about to let us out. She kept going on about how unseemly it was for us to be outside the walls. I was sure she'd been given instructions to keep us in and there was a hawk-like chowkidar or watchman at the gate to make sure we were. There was also Sohail.

Once I crossed through the courtyard in the late afternoon to find he had pulled their old TV set out of the sitting room. It wasn't so long ago TVs were banned in Afghanistan; maybe people like Mr Kumar kept them hidden until times changed. Men weren't usually in the house during the day, and I would have walked straight past, except I heard the words 'Steve Smith' and I stood still; not because I liked cricket but because I knew it was possibly in Australia.

Australia seemed so far away, but standing there like that, watching the green of the oval, I couldn't stop the tears rising up, blurring the screen and when I brushed them away, the camera gave a different view and I recognised it: the oval, the parklands, St Peter's Cathedral. 'It's Adelaide!' I didn't mean to move closer, but I did, scanning the crowd for a glimpse of someone I knew.

Sohail glanced at me. 'Ji. You know Adelaide?'

'It is my home town.' I hoped my voice was steady. Maybe I wasn't successful for Sohail's answer didn't come straight away; he looked up from the screen and my words hung in the air. Then he talked as if he were distracting an upset child.

'It is the fourth match. You like cricket?'

I was so surprised he spoke to me that I simply shrugged. Dad loved cricket. I grew up with it, but it didn't affect me. Yet, there I was, with my eyes glued to the screen. Australia was batting and the commentator was saying how Raza Hasan was pitching the ball too full on the leg side and how unhelpful that was because Steve Smith whipped it off his legs to the boundary.

'The Australians are strong on their leg side.' Sohail again. 'The bowler should have bowled a good length.'

I didn't care who was strong on their legs; I waited for the camera to scan the crowd again.

'Your country is very good,' Sohail conceded in the surprised respect a master uses to an apprentice.

'Do you think we'll win?'

He smiled, in sympathy. The respect didn't stretch that far.

There was another roar; Steve Smith was out. Smith was heading for a century too. 'This is a great series for Raza Hasan', and the Pakistani voice launched into a discussion with the Australian commentator of his past performance.

Maybe after that it was tea break, for Sohail gave me his full attention. It was the deepest conversation I ever had with him, even if the first part was about cricket. I lingered, wondering if more would be forthcoming, and amazingly it did. He told me about the night he abducted me, what they were saying in the van. He didn't actually apologise but I felt that's what he was trying to do. He told me how difficult it had been in their country, and still was. He had been conscripted by the Taliban—even kids as young as twelve were taken from their families to fight. He was glad to be back in the village now, living with his family in the way he should be. So many never returned.

I found myself wishing I could stay longer; there was so much I didn't understand. I wanted to ask why Sonya had to be abducted and when we'd be let go, but I could hear his mother calling me. Social customs there are so strict, and even though I thought it was ridiculous that you couldn't have a decent conversation with a guy without everyone thinking some chemistry was going to force you to rip your clothes off, the rules had to be obeyed. So I hurried off to see what she wanted.

We girls helped with all the jobs around the house. Mrs Kumar was always calling for us if we weren't within view. It was expected; the women worked so hard, and everyone did their share. That was how we found the solar oven. Liana and I were stacking boxes in a storeroom when she noticed the glazed glass top.

'Hey, Jaime!' I was right behind her. 'Isn't this one of those ovens made by the relief agency your uncle works for?'

It was. Apparently it'd been put away because no one had come to teach Mrs Kumar how to use it. Sonya was the biggest surprise of all. She even helped us pull it out into the sun. 'This is good,' she kept saying. 'With this style of oven the trees will not need to be cut for fuel, and kerosene is so costly.'

When we realised what she was talking about, Liana and I stared at her in surprise. It sounded like details Uncle Jon would say, not a girl that couldn't care less about Afghans. And when I suggested we show Mrs Kumar how to bake a cake in it, Sonya ran off to make arrangements.

'That's the first time I've seen her excited about anything,'

Liana commented. Nazira kept her usual sullen distance throughout the project.

'We must not trust Nazira,' Sonya said later, wiping flour off her nose. 'She acts strangely. She has never helped us in any of the ways Sohail said she would, nor does she like us. My Pakhtu is enough to speak with Mrs Kumar, so we do not need her help as a translator. Be careful of her.'

But even Nazira couldn't keep my spirits down. Apart from the worry about getting away and if Mum and Dad knew what happened to us, my immediate concern was Jasper.

Liana and I were sitting out in the courtyard waiting for the cake to cook. I don't know why we bothered; it took hours and hours in the winter sun. 'Li, Jasper bothers me.'

'Why?'

'I get the impression he thinks I'm naïve for trying to enjoy it here, but what can we do, after all? We're here so we have to make the best of it. I wish he'd relax. He's like a wolf, always on the prowl, shying away one minute, ready to fight the next. I wish I could hold him to let all his tension slip away.'

'He's a bit old for that,' Liana observed. 'In his present mood he'd take it the wrong way.'

I shrugged. 'Do you miss your family?'

'Sure, being here makes me want to see them.'

'Me too. Dad tried to warn me.' I sighed. 'I wonder what will happen.'

She seemed to follow my thoughts, knew I wasn't talking about Jasper or my family any more. 'I expect they'll let us go sooner or later.' I wondered if she believed it.

After lunch, when the household activities wound down

for a time of rest and Liana and I were in our room, I could hear 'Für Elise' again.

Whenever I heard it now, I could feel my head hurt. Soon the bell at the gate was ringing and servants rushed outside. I stayed at the window to see what the commotion was about. The children, who crowded around us that first day, appeared and were watching with awe on their dirty faces as a huge man unfolded himself out of a Suzuki van. I knew who it was. He was the sort of person you'd recognise from the next ridge on a mountain range.

I turned quickly at a sound behind me and Nazira sidled in with a satisfied smirk on her face. 'Mr Kumar has arrived.' Her whole demeanour spoke louder than her words: *Now we shall see what happens to you.*

Liana shivered after she'd gone. 'Is she ever a nasty piece of work. Wonder why she looked so smug.'

I was shaken too, and wondered what it was Nazira could know that we didn't. In Peshawar, Mr Kumar had been decent. Whether it was stupid or not, I still believed he wouldn't hurt us.

We didn't find out that day what would happen as we weren't sent for. It was Jasper who wasted no time in requesting an audience with the man. I personally thought he was rather heroic for braving the lion's den, but he told us he'd stewed long enough over whatever connection the Pakhtun had had with his father.

14

Jasper

When Jasper was let into the commander's den later that afternoon, he found it empty. He had an impression of a room that was surprisingly furnished in a mixture of West and East: a desk with the usual carpet cushions lining the walls. He moved over to look at the rugs scattered on the floor. There seemed too many, some piled on top of others. It was like a carpet shop. He dragged one back to see another underneath. He didn't like it very much—it had a modern design, stingers and Kalashnikovs with numbers pictured haphazardly. So garish. Who would buy such a thing?

He examined one designed like a map, yet it looked as though a bomb had blown the pattern to the four corners of the rug like fragments in a kaleidoscope. He frowned. It seemed to be telling some gruesome secret.

The commander surprised him as he entered. 'Admiring the rugs?' he said in Pakhtu

Jasper jumped. 'Not these,' he admitted truthfully.

The commander regarded him with something akin to respect in his eyes. 'They serve their purpose.' He sat on a cushion and leaned against another.

To Jasper's satisfaction Sohail walked in. Now he could kill two birds with one stone; he wished it wasn't just metaphorically.

'Assalamu Alaikum,' Sohail greeted him formally,

'Wa Alaikum Assalam,' Jasper answered through gritted teeth.

The commander motioned them to sit with him and, as Jasper perched on the edge of a cushion, he felt he was in a jirga, a formal tribal meeting.

'I hope you are having a pleasant stay in my home.'

Jasper caught the man eyeing him keenly, but he ignored his words. When he had something on his mind, Jasper didn't like to be deflected. He pulled out the orange-checked handkerchief from his pocket and held it so Sohail could easily see it.

'Where did you get this?' Jasper asked, hoping he was sounding mature with the right touch of authority in his tone.

Sohail moved closer to see. His mouth almost twitched into a grin as he recognised it, but sobered when he glanced at Jasper's face. He lifted his shoulders in an Afghan 'so be it' shrug. 'A friend of my father's left it here. I have used it ever since. I did not think he would have minded.'

Jasper turned to Mr Kumar. 'This belonged to my father.'

The commander leaned forward. 'Your father?' He scrutinised Jasper's features. 'Ji,' he murmured finally. 'That is it. There has been something about you from the beginning. So, Pembley Sahib.' He nodded as if he understood some puzzle at last.

Jasper stood, his body taut and shaking. 'I want to

know what happened to my father. What relationship did you have with him? You must tell me.' Jasper knew he'd spoken impolitely to one in a position of authority and he understood the swift anger that flashed across the older man's features. Anger he understood but not the pity and sadness that he thought he saw next. He let his gaze drop as the man let out a huge sigh.

'This has been a great source of sorrow for me also.'

Jasper's head jerked back to watch the commander.

'I know what happened to your father. Come, I will tell you.' He took Jasper to the window that looked out onto the stark mountains he'd travelled through to reach the village.

'See the road on the mountain up there? It is the road you came on a few weeks ago. Your father was coming here as he usually did—Ah, yes,' he answered Jasper's quick questioning look, 'he used to come. It was dangerous for him because he was American, but he came regardless. Your father was my good friend—he was the type of man one doesn't meet often in one lifetime. He told me many important things and I trusted his judgement. He taught our village the way of health. The bathroom you see in this house, the latrine outside, and the pump with which we draw our water from the well—all this is due to him. He saw to our sick and wounded also.' He sighed softly as Jasper shifted impatiently on his feet.

'Almost a year ago now, your father was on his way over those mountains … there was bombing, you understand—' Here the Pakhtun put an arm around Jasper's shoulders. Jasper wanted to shake it off but steeled himself to stand still. 'The van he was travelling in veered from the road and hit a mine.'

Jasper flinched. He'd thought it would be something like that, so why did he feel as though he was being told of his death for the first time?

'I am sorry, beta, my son. That is why there was no trace. His body was never found.'

Jasper clenched his teeth and stood away from him. 'Do you know what it's like never knowing what happened to someone you love?' He spoke in a low voice that threatened to crack. 'Why couldn't you have notified the authorities?'

'Your father and I spoke of this—what to do if anything should happen. You must understand—I was a mujahid when I was young, fighting a jihad to keep our country and religion safe. And now I command this area. Our country is still run by what the West calls a feudal system—the men under my jurisdiction will fight for me without argument. It would not have looked good on two counts if it were known your father was helping our village. People would say the relief agency he worked for had taken sides—they would have been in danger from other militant groups if it were made public. As would this village—we could have been a target also. The Taliban's influence has not vanished and there's a bigger threat arising—' He stopped, then murmured, 'So much hate.'

He glanced at Jasper. 'He talked about you, but I thought you were in America.'

'I was. I came back.' Jasper found he was breathing quickly, trying to stop the wave that was threatening to well up and destroy his credibility in front of these freedom fighters. He glanced up but couldn't handle the concern he saw on the older man's face. It made him feel vulnerable; at least when people looked at you with anger they didn't care what you were feeling. The man put a hand on Jasper's shoulder.

'Beta, you have to let this go now. This sorrow will weaken you.'

Jasper was tempted to shake off the man's touch and scream out that he wasn't his son. The only man who could lay claim to that title was dead. *Dead.* He shook his head in an effort to clear his thoughts and shut out the image he was seeing: the van and his father's body in little pieces. Instead he thought of Liana and Jaime. *The girls.* With embarrassment he realised he'd spoken aloud.

'Ah, those girls,' Mr Kumar mused. To Jasper he looked like a mountain lion watching deer at a waterhole.

'My wife has been telling me about them. And you are devoted to them, I hear. That is very commendable. You need not worry, appearances can be deceiving.' He leaned back against his table, arms folded. 'One of them is young to be sure, and maybe they know little of this world of war and its dangers, but within them is a strength that you know nothing of.'

Jasper stared at him, confused.

'Strength does not always show itself in brave words and deeds, beta. True strength comes from within, from faith—in God, in oneself, in others. It gives one the ability to come through turbulent waters and yet, remain calm.'

Calm was the last thing Jasper felt right then. Why was the commander talking about stuff like strength when he must know the girls needed protecting? Why had everyone, except him, forgotten about the abduction? At that moment, Jasper needed to be out of there and he stumbled as he turned. At least he was thankful to know what had happened, even glad his father didn't die in vain, but there was none of the peace of mind that he thought would come with the knowledge.

He stood still at the door a moment; then faced the Pakhtuns again. 'Will you tell me when we can leave this place?'

Mr Kumar smoothed his moustache with his middle finger. 'I am sorry, as yet, I cannot say. I must ask you to continue to trust my judgement.'

If Jasper hadn't already been reeling with the shock of finding out about his father, he might have laughed in the commander's face. Trust! What a joke, but he was too tired and left without another word.

That night, since Jasper couldn't sleep, he strolled outside. He'd stopped marvelling at the freedom he was given; he had realised that they knew he wouldn't leave without the girls. If it were different circumstances, he would have enjoyed the clear star studded sky and cold mountain air. A lone sheep bleated concern for a lamb; muffled sounds came from the bazaar as steel shutters were pulled down over shop stalls. Another day was over, but it was all lost on Jasper.

Inside him there was only room for a van careering down the mountain road. He saw the blast as it made impact, felt the heat of the fire and wondered how much you'd actually know or feel when you hit a mine. Would it hurt? Or would there be nothing? That he hadn't been there with his dad was more than just a regret; it was a feeling of disappointment so intense that it gnawed at his insides. What could he have done? At least now he knew how he died, but the healing didn't come.

God! he cried inside. *Why did you let it happen?* He kicked a stone viciously and the sound of it hitting the wall startled him out of his reverie.

Just then he heard another sound: that of someone pushing through the bushes on the other side of the wall. Lithe as a leopard, he jumped up and crouched on the wall. In front was a tree shading him from the moonlight but he could see a figure in a burqa hurrying down the narrow path through the field beyond. It had to be a woman and he gasped as she put up her hand to adjust her veil. The hand was white in the moonlight. Only three girls had skin as fair as that in the whole household—which one was it? He strained his eyes but it was no use, then decided that Liana was too sensible to do such a thing and although he thought Jaime might, there'd be no way she could have got out without knowing Pakhtu; the chowkidar looked too conscientious. It had to be Sonya.

She stopped to turn as if looking behind her; he shrank and stretched out in the shadows, imagining himself a stone. He held his breath as he gave her enough time to move forward. When he looked again, she was sitting, waiting. Shortly, a man, equally stealthy, approached her from the shadows beyond, and she stood, pulling up her burqa, her whole body poised for a joyful greeting. From his hiding spot, Jasper couldn't see the man's face, only that his hair looked pale in the moonlight. He watched them engaged in some urgent conversation, Sonya gesticulating towards the house, the man seeming to soothe her.

That was when an awful realisation hit Jasper. He'd suspected it all along but dreaded knowing for sure. For if he were right, it would mean danger for them all. There was no other explanation in his mind for Sonya's weird behaviour: she must be some sort of political agent!

15

Jaime

A few days after Mr Kumar arrived, Mrs Kumar took us girls out to the servants' quarters.

'She has a job for us,' Sonya explained. When we approached the meagre dwellings with rooms opening onto the courtyard, kids swarmed out like rabbits from a burrow at dusk.

'They don't have that many servants, do they? Look at all these kids.'

Sonya heard me. 'Many are orphans from camps set up nearby or from other villages. Some are relatives of people who have not yet returned from refugee camps in Pakistan, so the Kumars are offering shelter. So many are fatherless because of the conflict.' She sighed. 'There is a sick child Mrs Kumar wants us to see.'

'Why is it everyone thinks we know what to do just because we're from the West?'

Liana looked back at me. 'We most probably do know more than them. We can at least remember what our mothers did with us when we were sick.'

The child was lying on a charpai, a woven string bed,

so tired-looking, she didn't seem to have the energy to cry. After much questioning on Sonya's part, we discovered the child had severe diarrhoea. Even I could see if she wasn't treated soon, she'd die.

'They have stopped all food and drink so that she won't vomit any more,' Sonya stated.

'That doesn't sound right.' Liana sat on the bed and held the little girl's hand.

'Mum used to keep me drinking when I was sick like this,' I said. 'She gave me that oral dehydration stuff.'

'They won't have anything like that here.' Liana stroked the little girl's forehead.

I grabbed Liana's arm. 'Then we'll make some: water, sugar and salt. That's what it tasted like. And tell them to give her sips all day long.'

Sonya translated the recipe and soon the little girl was sipping from a chipped cup that an older girl held for her to drink. On the floor I noticed a piece of paper—a pencil drawing of a girl flying a kite, and where trees would have been, there were tanks. A hard lump rose in my throat. What had these kids been through? They had lost their parents, and only recently could they do ordinary kid-things like fly kites and dance or watch TV. Just then I felt a little hand creep into mine and I looked down to see a face grinning up at me. It was the little boy with the orange who had smiled the first day we came. He'd lost a tooth since then.

'Hello, how are you?' he said in English and giggled from behind his other hand.

Intrigued, I bent down beside him. 'You speak English?' His nod was probably just politeness for I couldn't get another word out of him. Sonya spoke to him in Pakhtu. Then I heard his reply, 'Harris Sahib.'

'Harris Sahib?' I exclaimed. 'Does he mean Jon Harris, the aid worker? Did he teach him those words? Has he been here?'

'I do not know. This boy comes from another village. Maybe he met the man there.'

'Ask Mrs Kumar. Please.'

Sonya hardly hesitated; she was more willing than she'd ever been. The longer we were in the village, the more humane she became. Soon she was back.

'Mrs Kumar said no Harris Sahib has been here. A different man came and taught the village to dig latrines and how to stay healthy. He brought the oven. But it was not Mr Harris. She doesn't know about the other village.'

It was weird. I had been happy enough up to that point, but hearing Uncle Jon's name like that (if it had been him) unsettled me, as though the rest of the world wasn't so far away after all, and maybe we should be doing more than sitting back, waiting to be set free. Maybe if I hadn't met that little boy, I wouldn't have been sucked in by Jasper's ideas.

Jasper found us there soon after. Apparently he'd been pacing around the kitchen door, waiting for permission to be let in to see us, when finally the cook had told him where we were.

'These Muslim households make it so difficult to get anything done,' was Jasper's first comment. He looked so irritable that I quickly asked him what was wrong.

'I want to talk to you both without Sonya, nor that snake, Nazira. She wouldn't let me in this morning.'

'Jasper, keep your voice down.' Liana and I led him to our part of the courtyard where we could be private. I braced myself inwardly for he looked more agitated than usual. 'Fire away,' I offered with a show of confidence I didn't feel.

'Last night, I couldn't sleep …' I relaxed and gave Liana a glance. Maybe this wouldn't be so bad after all. 'And I saw Sonya, outside the walls, meeting a European, maybe even a Russian.'

'You can't be serious!' But he was, very, and he told us everything, from his time in the war lord's office to seeing Sonya.

'Anyway it boils down to this—Sonya must be a spy.'

'She can't be,' broke in Liana. 'I've told you before, that problem with Russia is over.'

'Maybe she's a spy for the Afghan government. Maybe there's still some Russian influence that no one knows about. Maybe Afghanistan is trying to unite the central Asian states like Tajikistan to become part of Afghanistan, and Russia wouldn't want that to happen, would they? Who knows, maybe the Moscow government wishes they had those states back. And the pathway to a warm port.'

'Jasper, be reasonable, she's not much older than you. How—?'

'I tell you, she's up to something,' Jasper urged. 'I've suspected it for ages. All that business with the carpet shop in Islamabad, and then Peshawar. People believed the leadership for most of the Afghan resistance was based in Pakistan. Her father works for the embassy; she's got a perfect way to discover information and to pass it on. That must be why they kidnapped her, to stop her, and now that the commander's back, they'll be deciding what to do with her. And us.'

'Then how come they're so nice to us?' I asked.

'Jaime! Open your eyes.'

I wished he wouldn't get so annoyed, and so fast. He

made me jump when he burst into flames like that.

'That's so you won't suspect anything, or so we won't escape. They might even have other ideas. They're probably negotiating now about Sonya. And what about us? Perhaps they've already asked for money from an aid agency. These political groups always need money for their ammunition and weapons.'

I could tell Liana didn't believe him. She was pouting with scepticism. I wasn't so sure any more. Why had Sonya seemed so eager to find out if Jon Harris had been there?

'We have to escape—it's imperative—especially for your safety. Kumar may want Sonya alive but I'm sure they don't care a hoot about us—we just got in the way. If we don't do something soon, we'll just disappear off the face of the earth and no one will ever know what happened to us.' Jasper paused, emotion making his breath short and raspy.

'Jasper.' Liana moved closer to him. 'You don't have to be in control of everything. We will be looked after.' I stared at her; she had a point. I'd heard grief does strange things to your mind; I wondered if his near fanatical protection of us was connected to his dad's death. Liana was gentle, trying to stop him from worrying, so there was no warning of his reaction.

'Oh, no you don't!' And he slammed his hand hard against the wall, then turned to face her. 'Don't give me any of that crap of yours, Li, about a gracious Creator in control. There's no one in control of all this except ourselves. Yeah, I know this whole country believes in a merciful God, someone looking after things—well, they don't know much. A God that can let a man like Dad get blown up when he'd never done anything wrong, only good—'

Then he stopped like a steam train with an empty coal

shuttle. He wiped his hand over his forehead and sighed. 'I'm sorry. I really am.'

His voice grew soft and that was when I cried. I knew it would make him more determined to save us, but I could see an image of him dying inside. If only he could overcome the bitterness and hurt, maybe he'd see the world differently. I hugged him then. I hadn't done that since we were in Year 10 and I was leaving for Australia. I think he thought he was comforting me, but right then, he seemed like a child I had to cradle back to health.

He stood away from me and grasped both my hands; his eyes were too bright, like they'd been when he first spoke to me in the carpet shop in Peshawar. 'I'm sorry we're in this mess. But I'll make a plan and let you know what we can do.'

'Jas, when we go—we must take Sonya.'

'No!' He dropped my hands and I shut my eyes. I didn't think I could take it if he shouted again. 'She got us into this,' he added, more quietly.

Liana agreed with me. 'Please, Jas, she's just a girl, like us. She seems different now, and if what you say is true, then they'll get angry when we go, won't they? They might hurt her.'

'She'd get what she deserved, the little bitch.' He stood there staring at us. 'Oh, all right. But if she causes trouble, we dump her. I must be crazy, but seeing you smile like that is worth anything, I guess.' He was looking only at me then, and when he moved to go, his final words did the opposite of what he must have intended. 'I promise to get you out of this.'

Jasper's promise only made me uneasy, and I hoped with a passion almost matching his that the trembling in my middle was simply the fear of the unknown.

16

Jasper

Jasper wasted no time in thinking of a plan. He was sure he could get the girls out of the house at night. Sonya and Jaime looked much alike; Liana was taller and thinner, but he thought his plan would work. It was once they were outside the walls that the problems would begin. He decided a stroll in the bazaar might produce a few more ideas.

The village bazaar reminded him of the old parts of Peshawar with its noise and crowdedness. Little dingy shops sold almost everything from bicycle parts to eggs and buffalo milk. There wasn't as much food available as in the Peshawar shops, though, and in this bazaar, more space seemed to be given to copies of foreign weapons than to the staples of life. He watched the men making little round balls of dough in the hot tandoor shop and recognised the same kind of wheat bag that had been in the van all those weeks ago when they'd first arrived.

Next door was the hakim's surgery. Jasper hoped he never had to visit such a man. Half-baked doctors, they were called in Pakistan, giving out folk remedies that often didn't work when surgery would have been a better option. When all else failed, words from the Qur'an were written on little pieces of paper and put in a taveez, a type of locket around the patient's neck. Sometimes the paper was crushed up and swallowed.

A chai vendor offered Jasper a cup of his best. Jasper took in the rough-hewn tables filled with dented samovars and blue enamel teapots, and the shelves of little chipped teacups, upside down to dry. Men were already sitting on the raised carpeted platforms that took the place of Western tables, sipping chai and good-naturedly arguing. He liked teashops and their 'matey' atmosphere, and accepted thankfully, wondering if anyone knew who he was. The village wasn't so big that the men wouldn't notice a new face. He imagined they thought he was a guest of the Kumars. If only they knew.

He felt the tea seller's curious gaze on him but Jasper didn't want to tell anyone his fears, in case everyone supported whatever the commander did. He'd heard of villages just like this one where the khan or commander's word was law. Here, too, loyalty to Kumar seemed evident; he was what the American media would have called a war lord, yet Jasper hadn't heard a bad comment about him or his family in all the time he'd been there. It made him feel so alone, as though everything was closing in on him like dungeon walls in a video game. How could he possibly organise an escape? No one would be sympathetic.

He wandered on and paused at the opening to a primitive factory. Rows of young boys and a few older men sat on benches tying knots at the back of rugs stretched on huge wooden looms. Curious, yet knowing the answer, Jasper asked the nearest boy what he was making.

'A rug, of course,' one little boy answered with a 'don't

you have eyes?' edge to his tone. Apparently it was thanks to Mr Kumar's goodwill that the factory was started, to create job opportunities for the villagers and for those from surroundings areas who had lost their families. There were more such projects, Jasper was told. The commander was a good man; he thought of his people. He let the boys in the rug factory have exercise during the day and time off to study. He even provided the patterns for the carpets, one boy told him, and that saved much time. Jasper couldn't stomach hearing more about the commander's good works. The people were brainwashed, he was sure of it. Most of the war lords he'd heard about were siphoning off the aid from the West into their own pockets.

Deep in thought while crossing the street, Jasper was startled by the sound of close rifle fire. A Pakhtun horseman rode recklessly past him, rifle in the air, shouting like a madman. He reined in his horse in a stone-scattering skid at the hakim's surgery and struggled to pull a man-sized bundle from the front of his saddle. Soon a crowd formed, and many hands helped to lift the wounded man down. Other spectators were quick with questions and advice. Jasper joined the mob, trying to hear what had happened. He only caught snatches but it was enough.

'—no horse. Not a hope.'

'Mujahideen from the fort … may Allah in his wisdom cut off their—'

Jasper watched, mesmerised, as the blood dripped to the ground, making a trail from the horse to the hakim's room. How could he ensure that his own escape party wouldn't run into a bigger danger once they were away from the village? The idea came to him then. Horses! He had to get horses. But how? There were hardly any left—they'd been conscripted by fighters. Even if he could find some, they couldn't ride the same animals all the way to Peshawar. Kabul wasn't so far away, but that was too dangerous; even the UN couldn't always get relief through the area because of renewed militant activity. He knew he had to think of a plan and how to do it without anyone telling Sohail or Kumar.

ﻋﻠﻰ

When he returned to the house, Sohail had an invitation for him. 'There is a betrothal party in the village tonight, my friend. Come with me.'

Jasper bit back a retort that he wasn't Sohail's friend. He didn't want to go anywhere with Sohail, nor was he fooled by the invitation. No doubt it was an easy way for Sohail to keep an eye on him. Even though he didn't like the young Pakhtun, he tried to be civil. He had enough sense to realise that while he was being cooperative he would be allowed more freedom, and freedom was what he needed if he were to organise an escape.

The party was for men only and although alcohol was forbidden the men had as much fun as guys do at drunken bucks' parties in Australia. As usual, they had their firearms with them and discharged them into the air, whooping as if they were totally off their faces.

'All in fun,' Sohail explained, smiling at them like an indulgent schoolteacher with a group of restless boys. 'See that boy sitting over there? That's the groom.'

Jasper noticed the boy's youth and nervousness with compassion, the same age as himself. 'He looks young for marriage.'

Sohail laughed. 'Boys are born men in Afghanistan.' Then he sobered as he faced Jasper. 'Here, we fight, even though the rest of the world is sick of hearing about us, hoping that if they do not know, then the fighting will be finished. It is good to marry young because as boys fight, they become men quickly. Here, they don't grow old—they die young.'

Jasper remembered the scene in the village that day. 'This morning I saw …' he began.

'That boy was the same age as you, Jasper. I saw him too. Was he not a man? If he was old enough to die for his people, was he not old enough for a woman?'

All at once the noise grew louder as men milled around Sohail, drawing him into a dance. One man played a rabaab, his fingers racing and jumping on the strings. Another played the beat on the tablas. The other men were joking and Sohail laughingly joined in, his earlier intensity apparently forgotten. The men beckoned to Jasper too. 'Come, we can dance again,' they said. But he was not in the mood for dancing and moved away from the revelry, closer to the shadows. He just wanted to think.

Suddenly he felt a hand grip his shoulder. Instinctively he turned, but the fingers dug in so that he stood still. 'Don't move!' came a low order in English. 'Act normal.' Jasper dropped slowly back into the dark.

'Who are you?' Jasper tried to keep his head to the front as if he were watching the dancing.

'I am a journalist from CNN,' the voice replied. 'I have come to get you out. It took an age for me to find you.'

'How did you know who I was?' Jasper wasn't sure if he should trust the man. His accent was vaguely familiar.

'Don't be stupid, kid. Your face is all over the papers in the subcontinent. Do you still have the Russian girl with you?'

'Yeah, and the Australian girls too.'

The man swore under his breath, as if he were calculating a situation he hadn't expected. 'Okay, I suppose we should take you all at once.'

Jasper tried to breathe normally. If this was the escape route he was hoping for, it seemed too easy.

'You will need to get out of the village by yourselves. Two kilometres down the road, there is a waterfall. I will wait for you with a jeep at two each morning. Then we shall get you out of this godforsaken hole.'

Jasper thought a journalist should be a little more encouraging; he didn't sound sympathetic at all, but then maybe the man was just tired from tracking them down. How did he find them anyway?

'Wait. Who shall I say, if I have to ask for you?'

'You won't have to. I'll be there tomorrow night and the next. If you don't show, we'll think of something else. But try and do it, kid. We don't have forever.'

As suddenly as he had appeared, the journalist was gone. Jasper wasn't sure whether to be glad for a solution or worried about the strangeness of it. He jumped when Sohail found him, puffing slightly.

'The dancing good?' Jasper thought he'd better make some comment, but then wished he hadn't as his voice wasn't steady.

'Are you feeling well, Jasper?'

'Sure.' It was disturbing how nothing seemed to escape Sohail's notice. He'd have to be careful.

Just then, some of Sohail's friends brushed past. 'Hoi,

Sohail—enjoying some last freedom, eh?' Sohail didn't answer. The other boys were in high spirits and the sound of their voices floated back loudly enough for even Jasper to understand their meaning. One of them was explaining. 'It will be Sohail's turn next. I hear he will marry a foreign girl, the lucky devil.' The rest was lost in bawdy laughter, but Jasper had heard enough. He tried to breathe normally as he faced Sohail. So that was it, was it? It couldn't be Sonya. What Afghan would marry a Russian?Liana and Jaime! In that culture even Jaime at sixteen wasn't too young for marriage. He'd heard of Jihadist fighters forcing girls to be their wives while they fought. He had hoped the Kumars were better than that.

He forced himself to calm down as he knew he couldn't give the game away or he'd ruin their chance of escape. Sohail acted as though he hadn't heard the comments at all and Jasper tried to follow his example.

'I think it is time we returned to the house. Shall we go, my friend? We can see the outcome of the one-day match between Australia and West Indies. Steve Smith is one of the world's top batsmen.'

Jasper tipped his head, even though he hated cricket and didn't care who Steve Smith was. It wasn't even worth challenging Sohail on the use of the word 'friend'.

17

Jaime

One morning, when Jasper came to tell Liana and me we needed horses to escape, I showed enthusiasm for the idea at first. I guess it was the thought of the horses.

'It'll be no picnic, Jaime,' he warned. 'And I'm not sure of all the details yet, but we will need to pay for the horses. Enough to speak louder to any seller than a punishment from the commander.'

'You mean a bribe? That doesn't usually work for long; they'll tell the same information to someone else for more than you gave them.'

'Not a bribe—payment.' He hesitated. 'I have this old cross of Mum's, which I only wear because Dad had one the same.' I leaned closer as he pulled it out from under his long shirt. It was quite large and looked Celtic, but it was something a Westerner would appreciate, not an Afghan. 'It's only silver,' he murmured finally. 'It wouldn't buy the tail of a horse.'

There was a rather unhappy silence as I did some quick thinking. I knew my bangle would buy enough horses for a cricket team. 'I do have this bangle,' I finally said.

'I know.' Jasper's voice was gentle, in the way he used to talk to me when we were younger. He stood there in front of me, looking miserably at the bangle. 'I understand how much it means to you. And I would never ask this, except it is life or death.'

'Yeah, I know.'

He picked up my hand then and held it tight. 'Jaime, look at me.' And he lifted up my chin. 'If we get out of this, I'll get you another one. Somehow.'

I knew he meant it, and I appreciated what he tried to do, but it wasn't just the bangle. I kept seeing Uncle Jon's face the day he gave it to me and I realised that deep down, I'd hoped that Uncle Jon would rescue us. He worked in Afghanistan; he knew many of these villages. I'd imagined our escape would come from him; giving up the bangle was like giving up that hope as well.

As I looked up at Jasper I wondered if my hopelessness showed because he drew me towards him and held me. 'Don't worry.' His voice was calm then, little more than a whisper, but I could feel the tension in his body as if he were ready to spring. 'I'll get us out of here.'

Liana tried to talk him out of it, saying how dangerous it would be, but he was pumped up, even excited that something was happening at last, and suddenly I gave in. I'd never been able to better him in arguments or games when we were kids, and lately he was like a consuming fire, eating all my attention and willpower. I stood back and started unclasping the bangle, but he reached out and covered my hands with his own.

'Jaime.' The intensity in his tone as he said my name

stilled me. 'You won't regret this.' I stood there, stunned, as he took the bangle from my arm himself. His words were ordinary in themselves but he'd made them sound as though he'd said he cared for me. Really cared, as if I were special. I'd caught a glimpse of the Jasper I knew as a child, but there was a difference—we were older now. What would his care mean now?

Liana was asking him questions then and he told us the basic plan for getting out of the grounds.

'By the way, how's your friend Sonya?' I looked up at the touch of sarcasm, as Liana answered him and I hoped he wouldn't baulk at taking Sonya as well.

'She's acting funny, a bit jumpy. And Nazira stalks around as if looks could kill, and we don't know why.'

'Well, tell Sonya we'll go as soon as I say the word.' It was surprising but it lifted my spirits. Perhaps he was feeling better. Since he was leaving, I tried to make light of the situation. I grinned at him as he paused at the door, and I tried to sound happy. 'Just get me a horse that doesn't buck, okay?'

He gave a short laugh. That was worth hearing. Then he saluted as he left.

At the end of the day, Sohail managed to find me in the courtyard to tell me Pakistan had won the latest test. He must have thought I'd be interested. 'Pakistan and Australia have two matches each. Now the series will be determined by the last test.' His face showed his satisfaction with how the cricket was going, but all I could think was how nice it would be to have no worries beyond the outcome of a game. He didn't linger and sauntered off to find Jasper.

Liana and I had just described to Sonya Jasper's plan of getting over the wall. I was surprised that she seemed so relieved. Being Sonya, I thought she'd disagree with some detail, if not the whole idea.

'I thought you liked it here,' I asked her.

'I do. It is just that it has to happen sometime—my—um, our escape.'

That was when I truly wondered if Jasper was right about her, after all. She left the room then to find Mrs Kumar. She spent more time with the lady of the house than we did and I guessed it was because they could speak the same language. I soon forgot about Sonya. We were tidying up after dinner when I noticed an odd detail on one of the rugs.

'Do you know, Liana, some of these carpets are weird. See this?' I put down the dishes and ran my fingers over the red woollen weave.

'This is an elephant foot design, but it hasn't got the full traditional pattern. Here it looks as if a word is woven into the weave between the flowers instead of the usual geometric design. And see this? On a lot of Afghan rugs there's a symbol like a dollar sign, except it doesn't mean that, of course. But in this pattern it looks as though Persian numbers are following the sign as if it really is an amount of money.'

Liana didn't answer me. I was disappointed at her lack of interest, until I heard a slight moan.

I swung my head up to look at her. 'Li?'

'It's my stomach. Headache.' She groaned. 'Dizzy too.'

'Let's get you to bed, then.' I helped her into our room and onto one of the beds.

'I can't be sick. Jasper's wild escape will happen soon. You know what he's like lately, when things don't go as planned.'

'Don't worry, I'll try to unearth some medicine.'

'Yuck. The medicine for this is worse than being sick.'

I had to smile; now Jasper's escape plan wouldn't just be play-acting.

18

Jasper

Jasper walked through the bazaar to the village stables. It wasn't a problem buying four horses, but securing the stable hand's silence was difficult.

'This is too much trouble,' the man said. 'One gold bangle is not enough.'

Jasper bit on it and motioned to the man to do the same. 'It's good gold,' he argued. 'Enough to buy five horses and you know it.'

Greed finally got the better of the man as Jasper hoped it would, and he reluctantly agreed.

'I'll be here at eleven tonight. Make sure the horses are ready to go.' Jasper was glad it wasn't the month of Ramadan when there would have been people on the streets, celebrating and eating throughout the night. Then he would never have managed to get the girls away without being seen.

Jasper usually felt better when he had a plan of action, but that day, even on the street in broad daylight, he was uneasy. He glanced behind him often as he wouldn't have put it past Sohail to have him followed. It would be simple in that little bazaar; shops sprawled out onto the narrow road and vendors crowded around calling out their wares. One man shoved a shawl in Jasper's face in hope of a sale, just as Jasper was trying to check behind him. Finally, he decided it was his own fears making him jumpy, and he made his way back to the house to tell the girls that everything was set for that evening.

He stationed himself outside the kitchen door, waiting for Mrs Kumar to come out of the ladies' side of the house. He always had to ask permission to go into the women's quarters and, even though he knew it was the custom, the waiting frustrated him. 'I would like to see my sisters please,' he asked when she finally emerged. He was certain that she believed him to be the girls' brother or she wouldn't have allowed him such liberties.

'I am sorry, you cannot today,' she said pleasantly. 'One of them is quite ill.'

Jasper's heart sank. 'Please, Mrs Kumar. I must see them.' And try as he did, he couldn't keep the agitation out of his voice. Even to his own ears he sounded demanding. Mrs Kumar's smile vanished. Fortunately, it seemed she had misinterpreted his real intent, but it didn't stop him feeling like a goat on the butcher's block.

'I do not like your manner, young man. If I say you will not see the girls, then you will not. I see you have been given too much licence. You should keep away from this side of the house for a few days until you cool down.' With a flick of her shawl she entered the kitchen, turning only to give him a frown, as he stood there wondering what to do next.

He plunged his hands into his vest pockets and paced the kitchen garden. The front gate squeaked open as a servant brought produce from the bazaar. That was it! He felt in his pocket for his pencil stub. He'd write them a note. He thought it would be safe since Sohail was hardly ever in the house during the day and no one else would be able to read English. Hurriedly he scratched a message on the back of a receipt he'd received in the bazaar and knocked on the kitchen door. It opened slowly and the servant stood there, a leer spreading over his features.

'What do you want?'

Jasper swallowed, hoping his scheme would work. The servant didn't seem very receptive. 'I see you have fruit from the bazaar. Could I ask you to take some to my sister? She's sick.'

The servant leaned against the doorpost. 'I have oranges, but I do not take orders from you.'

Jasper dug into his shalwar pocket and drew out a few afghanis. This wasn't going as well as he had hoped. 'Of course, I'm willing to pay for them.' And he held out the notes.

'They cost more than that. It is hard to get oranges these days.'

Jasper bit his tongue. The amount he was offering was much more than they were worth, but he took out more money. 'Can I see the oranges? Since I'm paying the moon for them, the least you can do is let me pick them out.'

The man grudgingly brought a bag of oranges and a basket, and Jasper took a few out of the bag and put them into the basket while slipping the note underneath so it wouldn't be seen. 'These are fine.' And he forced himself to smile.

'To your sister, eh?' The servant grinned at him with a wink, and Jasper instantly stilled. What did the man suspect? He felt as though the whole household knew what he was planning. Worried, Jasper waited out of sight, under the window to see if the oranges got further than the kitchen. He heard Nazira go in and bang a tray down on the table.

'Why do you look so stupid?' Her voice was caustic and Jasper almost felt sorry for the servant, if that was what he had to put up with every day. The man didn't seem offended though.

'That Angrez wants to give his sick sister oranges. I have never seen a more devoted brother,' and he laughed at his innuendo.

'So he should be. Here, give me that basket and I will see that the girl gets it. It has been nothing but work, work, work ever since they came.'

Nazira must have left the kitchen then. She sounded sincere enough, but Jasper wasn't happy. Would that basket of fruit be safe with Nazira?

19

Jaime

I was sitting on Liana's bed when Nazira came in with a basket of oranges from Jasper.

'How is the sick one?' she asked, sounding as if she really wanted to know. I was still picking up my chin from the floor when she put the oranges beside Liana on the bed. She didn't even dump them down as she usually did with our food. 'Your brother hopes you will enjoy these oranges. He is sorry you are sick.' She managed to look as if she cared.

'Thank you, Nazira,' Liana said, as surprised as I was.

'Wonder what's got into her,' I murmured.

'Goodness knows.'

'Hey, here's a note sticking out. It's from Jasper.'

'What's it say?'

'Oh, Li.'

Liana pulled herself up further on the bed. 'What's wrong?'

'We have to go tonight.' I grabbed her hand. 'How can we do that when you're so sick?'

Liana struggled to sit up properly. 'I'll be okay by then. Don't stress.'

I went and stood by the window. 'It even looks as though it could rain.' Suddenly, a thought struck me and I went back to Liana. 'You don't suppose Nazira saw the note, do you? It was sticking out for anyone to see.'

Liana shook her head. 'It wouldn't matter even if she did. Jasper wrote it in English—she wouldn't be able to understand it.'

I sank on to the bed again, staring out through the window at the clouds curling in the sky. It was like a moment of reckoning before a huge race; except this time our life depended on our winning. I could imagine Jasper being ready to take a risk. Normally I wouldn't mind the risk of danger too; I'd taken plenty with Dad. I guess that was the difference; if Dad or Uncle Jon were with us, I would have felt braver. There were so many things that could go wrong, and what would we do once we were out of the village?

'I know this sounds stupid, Li, but I feel safe here. No one has hurt us. We haven't been threatened.'

'Yeah. I just hope Jasper knows what he's doing.'

'It's scary because if we choose the wrong way, it'll be our fault.'

'I don't think we should worry. Even if things don't turn out the way we want, surely something positive can come of it.'

Liana often amazed me. Here she was, cheering me up, when she must have felt dreadful. She sat up against a cushion.

'Jaime, I really should tell you a story.' She looked almost well again and a pink flush grew in her cheeks.

I held my breath in excitement. Liana, being a quiet person, usually didn't disclose details about her personal life. 'About the time you were with Mr Kimberley when we were taken hostage during the terrorist attack?'

She nodded and started from the beginning. That's the way we spent the hours until the time came to make our escape. I'll never know if it was a way for her to help me forget what was coming, or whether she felt she had to tell it in case it all went wrong that night and the story would never be told. Whatever the reason, I'm glad she did. I'd never understood before how people can do unexpected things in a time of crisis. The story gave me a part of her that I would never have had otherwise.

It made me think of Dad and Mum too. What if Jasper's plan did go wrong? We could tread on a mine for starters. Would I ever see my family again? Elly with her little mice, quiet and clever Andrew. What were they thinking? Surely the school or one of the embassies would know by now that we were missing. They would have told Mum and Dad. It would be impossible to keep Dad off the next flight. He would have been looking for an excuse to come. Surely Uncle Jon would find out about us? He had contacts in Afghanistan and had permission to cross the border. He'd know where the most dangerous fighting was, the mines, the mujahedeen who were friendly and those who weren't.

I rested on the bed near Liana, imagining my own story—how Uncle Jon would take Dad across the border as his driver because Dad's dark hair, olive skin and green eyes made him look Afghan, especially in a shalwar qameez and turban. Fortunately, he still had his beard. At the check posts, he'd have to be quiet and act like a driver. *Oh Dad, I wish you were here.*

20

Jaime

That evening, Sonya, Liana and I prepared ourselves. I stuffed the blue burqa under my Afghan dress but kept my sneakers on in case there would be lots of walking, and the others followed suit. Fortunately, our burqas were the same colour. Jasper's plan wouldn't have worked, otherwise. Any little noise made us jump; it felt as if everyone in the house could hear what we were doing as we waited fully clothed under our quilts for Mrs Kumar to retire. Mrs Kumar often slept in our room and that night she seemed to take an age to settle. We had ideas about what to do if Nazira caused us any problems, but amazingly enough, she had disappeared.

Finally, the sound of regular breathing came from Mrs Kumar's bed and, in relief, we crept out of our warm quilts. Just before we reached the kitchen door, Sonya grabbed hold of my arm and whispered, her voice tense and raspy in the stillness of the room, 'If I get parted from you, there will be no need to worry. Do you understand?'

'That won't happen.' I tried to sound reassuring.

'Please, just in case it does.'

'Okay.' I humoured her, because I knew it wouldn't happen, not with Jasper in top form. For one of those split seconds, which seem longer in moments like that, I stared at her, marvelling at how she'd changed, and yet there seemed no reason for it. She seemed to trust that Jasper knew what he was doing. She hadn't asked how we knew his plan either, nor questioned it. She was never with us whenever he visited, so maybe she assumed he told us personally.

Liana was holding up reasonably well and I told Sonya to start. 'You first. Remember what to do?'

Sonya put on her burqa, ducked out the door like a blue ghost and scuttled into the outside toilet. The night watchman had just appeared from around the front, doing his rounds. He saw her, and he seemed satisfied that all was well. I grinned at Liana. Everything was going to plan. Sonya's pretended moans of agony drifted back across the lawn. I checked my watch. Right now, while Sonya was keeping up the act, she would be pushing out the narrow high window that I'd loosened earlier that day. Then the plan was that she would heave herself up to squeeze through onto the wide stone wall. Jasper would be waiting below.

I waited for the appointed five minutes before running for the outhouse in my burqa. I wasn't as fortunate as Sonya. Jasper must have miscalculated the night watchman's round, unless the man had cut it short for some reason, as halfway across the lawn I heard the command to stop. I turned to look around; I had no peripheral vision in the burqa. I could just make out the man's form coming towards me. I measured the distance to the wall in front of me and decided it was too risky to run for it; Liana still had to come. I turned to face him fully, blinking at the glare as he lifted his lantern high. I wondered if he could see my eyes through the mesh. It was nerve-wracking—I never expected to be inspected through the burqa, but I said the words Jasper had taught us to say if we were stopped, 'Peta kharab shuay. My stomach has a problem.'

The chowkidar grunted and let me pass while he continued his beat around the grounds. I was hoping he thought Sonya had also been me; maybe the plan had worked so far, but I didn't relax until I shut the toilet door behind me. The idea was to wait for Liana, to help her up. I peered out through a crack in the door and could just make out her shape leaning against the kitchen door frame. She was supposed to move five minutes after me, but she didn't come. She was still there, leaning against the door. Then she missed the next round of the night watchman's beat as well. Time was running out, but I didn't dare call to her.

Suddenly, I sensed rather than heard a movement in the house. Liana must have heard it for she ran out blindly—right into the arms of the chowkidar! I could hear his words as he spoke to her, but couldn't understand, and I began to panic for I knew Liana didn't speak much Pakhtu either. I opened the door a little, straining to see. She looked like a limp doll that was about to fold over any minute. The man shone the lantern peering at her as he did me, and I heard his sudden intake of breath. We didn't look alike—her eyes were brown—surely he would know something was up. But he waved her on.

علم

I opened the door wider. 'Hurry, Li.' My whisper sounded louder in my halfway state between fear and excitement. 'We've lost time.'

She sat down, out of breath. 'It worked, Jaime. I think he thought we were all the same girl. Just like Jasper said he would.'

I grunted. Privately I thought it was because, even in the burqa, she looked so sick. No one could mistake the stoop and faint moans that stomach cramps brought.

'Oh,' she groaned. 'How am I going to get up there?'

'It'll be easy.' I said it with a confidence that I didn't feel. 'Here, give me your hand and I'll pull you up. Hurry, the chowkidar might send a serving girl to check on you.'

After many scratches and much grunting, Liana was sitting unsteadily on the wall beside me.

'Jasper!' I whispered into the dark below me. 'We're here. Take Li.' I heard scraping on the wall and then his head and shoulders appeared, silhouetted against the skyline. He wore the wrapped turban of the men in the bazaar and for an instant I thought we'd been sprung.

Then he spoke, 'I hope she can ride.'

'I'll be okay,' Liana said. 'I'll hold on tight.'

'Make sure you do, and yell if you need to stop. Okay?' Liana disappeared into the darkness as Jasper carried her to one of the horses.

Soon, Jasper was helping me down. He had put rocks for stepping-stones at the base of the wall and as he stepped backwards, I felt him move slightly, as if he were losing his footing. For an instant before he steadied himself, I felt his weight come against me, pushing me to the safety of the wall. I guess that was when I first wondered where our childhood friendship might have ended up, if I hadn't returned to Australia. He'd been angry lately, but it was good seeing him like this, with his aggression put to good use.

Then I realised my feet were on the ground and I remembered in time to let go of Jasper's neck. 'Is that white horse for me?' Even though the moon wasn't out yet, I could see how special the animal was.

Jasper was right behind me, speaking softly, so that I wondered if the moment on the wall had affected him as well. 'I'm sorry about the colour—not such a good idea for a getaway at night, but the stable guy switched it at the last moment. Said the one I chose needed a new shoe. Didn't think they fussed much about shoeing horses here, but there wasn't time to argue. Think you can handle him?'

'Sure. He's awesome, like he's dancing in the moonlight.' I mounted (really difficult in a burqa) and leaned forward from the saddle to pat the side of the horse's neck. 'Hello, Moondancer.' Little beads, bells and coins were threaded onto the bridle and when he tossed his head and stepped forward, the chinking of the ornaments beat out a rhythm that I hoped wouldn't carry far in the night air.

Jasper gave a low call to all three of us. 'Let's go. We need to be at this meeting place early.'

There was little movement in the bazaar as we trotted through. All the shops were shuttered early during the winter months in villages like these and we didn't draw attention from any of the few men walking home along the road. Jasper, dressed in tribal clothes with the turban wrapped around his head, looked just like any other Pakhtun riding out at night, and the burqas were an excellent disguise for us girls.

Once on the road, we urged the horses into a canter, and the bushes and wispy trees, newly planted, steadily dropped behind. I prayed we wouldn't find a mine. Surely they would be cleared from the roads first, but Uncle Jon had told me once that it was easy to miss a mine that had become buried over the years.

Soon, drops of rain gave warning to pull the burqa over my face. I'd gratefully lifted it after we left the village. For a while, it seemed as if we were riding blindly. I could see Jasper's shape in front of me but that was all. Liana was still holding on beside me and I couldn't see Sonya.

Then, as instantly as the rain began, there was a lull, and a break appeared in the clouds ahead. I could see Jasper glancing behind him. Surely no one could be following us in that weather. I guessed he was checking on us. I was thinking what a pity it didn't rain more—maybe the drought would break.

It seemed a long time before Jasper slowed his horse, and then I could hear the sound of trickling water. He seemed to know where we were headed. I pulled on the reins with a whinny from Moondancer as he shifted his feet and tossed his head. Jasper shouted and the wind whipped his words back to us. 'We won't stay here. We'll go up the ridge and wait for the guy.'

What guy? I wondered, but it wasn't the time to ask. Jasper would never hear me and I pulled Moondancer around to follow him. It was difficult encouraging the horses up the steep incline but finally we were standing above what would have been a sizable waterfall, if there wasn't a drought. I could only see three horses as we tied them to the branches of some thick bushes, then suddenly, Sonya appeared on foot. I wanted to ask where her horse was, but Jasper began talking. 'You girls need to stay here. I'll scout around a bit, check where this guy is. Don't show yourselves until I return or I call. Okay? Just in case there's a problem.'

I helped Liana down and we were sitting under one of

the bushes when Jasper came to check on us before he left. 'How's the tum, Li?'

'A bit better. The ride did me good, believe it or not.'

Jasper bent down and touched my face. It was the kind of caress a guy gives a girl when he's about to kiss her. Jasper didn't kiss me, but it felt as if he had. I sat there in the cold, stunned, as I watched his shape shimmer out of sight.

Growing up in a co-ed boarding school made you grow close to guys, but it was a closeness that was like family. It had to be like that, or you'd be falling for every guy you spent too much time with. Yet, it was weird how just one year away could break the cycle for me. I found myself thinking of Jasper the way any other girl in Australia would see him: good looking and interesting. I could see that he still cared, but I guessed it was the friendly type of comradeship we'd shared as kids. I was glad, for I thought we'd lost even that.

I wished I could show him that I cared too. If only he was happier, but I knew that he was the one who had to let that happen. All I could do was accept him, moods and all.

21

Jasper

The rain stopped and the wind began to die down. Jasper trudged up the slope, finding it difficult to see ahead. Nothing seemed unusual to him, and as far as he could tell, there was no jeep nestled anywhere. He was early—he'd planned it that way—yet he felt unnerved. He was on the windward side of the waterfall gully by then and knew the girls wouldn't be able to hear him, even if he shouted, so he turned to go back, pausing to listen for sounds from the road below.

Instantly, he sensed a presence. Was that a stone scattering? He whirled around, but he was too late! A body sprang out of the bushes with the force of a leopard, and hurled itself onto him. Jasper felt the jolt down his spine as his back slammed onto the stony ground. Jasper's relief that it was not an animal was short-lived, for a man was soon astride him, holding him to the ground. Chest heaving, and fear giving him extra strength, Jasper strained to throw the man off. He wasn't strong enough.

Jasper pulled an arm free and hit out with his fist, hearing the man grunt as the blow must have smashed into his face. The man loosened his grip and it was all Jasper needed. With a roar, he flung his attacker back and threw himself on him. All the pent-up anger and frustration of the past weeks, even months, combined with an instinct to protect, drove him.

The mist lifted and the two rolled over, down the rise, each trying to master the other. Rivulets of sweat ran down the inside of Jasper's shirt. His heart pounded. He knew he had to win. If the guy was from the fort, even the girls would be in danger.

In the clearing night mist, Jasper saw the glint of steel near his face. He felt sick as he thought he'd been close to overpowering the guy. But how could he fight against a knife? He hadn't any experience with weapons. He knew by then the man had to be a militant. So this was how it would end. He'd heard what some militants did to their victims before they killed them. With that thought, Jasper struggled harder, trying to force the knife away, but his attacker's grip was like iron. He could feel his arm being pushed down as the knife drew closer. He closed his eyes and felt the sharp point touch his neck.

'I will not use this on you, my friend.' From above him the words came between ragged breaths.

Jasper's eyes flew open. He hardly dared to believe his ears as he understood the familiar Pakhtu, and he strained to see into the darkness.

'Sohail? You almost killed me!'

'I did not,' returned the other. 'I had to stop you only. Talking to you does little good at all.'

'Can you get off me? I can hardly breathe.'

Sohail sheathed his knife, kneeling back from Jasper as the

younger boy sat up, feeling his neck, and adjusting his eyes to the light and shadows that the rising moon was casting across the ground. Jasper didn't need to see the way Sohail held himself to know he was still angry. He could feel it, as if he could reach into the air and touch it; yet he ventured a question.

'How did you find me?'

Sohail laughed but it was the mirthless response to a fool trying to be clever. 'Do you think you could have left our village, if we did not let you go?'

Jasper could see it then; it had been too easy, but still he asked, 'What do you mean?'

'We let the stable boy give you the horses. He valued his life too much not to tell me about your visit. Of course, I changed one of the horses for my white stallion so I could easily follow. I had to come after you. It was necessary—for Sonya's safety. She had to escape, certainly, but not your way.'

'But …'

'Then I found out late tonight that you had been contacted by an agent.'

'If you mean that guy at the party, you're wrong. He's a journalist.'

'He was not what he said he was. They are very clever. He comes from Moscow.'

'Are you sure?' Even as he asked, Jasper was remembering the guy's accent at the party. Come to think of it, he did sound like Sonya.

'I am sure. About everything.'

Jasper was very still. 'And I gave Jaime's bangle for those horses. All for nothing!'

'I am sorry I could not retrieve your payment. The stable boy had already passed it on.'

'Then I must get back to the girls.'

Sohail's tone was smooth, almost friendly again. 'Do not worry. It has been taken care of—the man will not come. He is, at present, in our storeroom. Only Nazira knows he is there.'

Jasper began remembering then; Sonya outside the walls, meeting someone; Sonya in Islamabad, in the embassy car. 'I don't get this—what's going on? Who is Sonya, anyway?'

Sohail sat still for so long that Jasper thought he hadn't heard. 'Sonya had to escape to show she was not one of us,' he finally said. 'It would have saved her life. But this man you spoke to—he would say he caught her working for us. He used you as jackal bait, my friend. Tonight he would have ambushed you, and Sonya would have been in danger. She would be guilty in their eyes.'

It was just a riddle to Jasper. His head spun as he tried to piece Sohail's words into logical threads. When they wouldn't make a pattern, he thought the Pakhtun must have invented it so they wouldn't make the rendezvous.

'It is not just Sonya,' Sohail carried on. 'What do you think would have happened to the other girls? Jaime looks so like Sonya that these men would have shot her as well to be sure they got the right one.' Maybe Sohail sensed Jasper's confusion and disbelief because he explained further.

'These times are difficult. The rest of the world thinks we have been given our freedom, but there is no peace. Everyone is still fighting. The West thinks they are helping this party and that one; they provide money, arms, even men to find out secrets. The secret is passed on but it has already been bought for a higher price.'

'I don't—'

'And you ...' Sohail bent closer and regarded Jasper in the rising moonlight. 'These are dangerous times. Why did you not think? Why did you not ask from Khuda His will? You would have been told it was foolish to trust such a man. You were leading those girls to certain death!'

'H–how can you say that? You're a Muslim. That's not your kind of prayer, is it?'

Sohail smiled. At least Jasper thought it was a smile; he could see white shining in Sohail's face.

'Ji, you are right, I am Muslim. I will never turn my back on hundreds of years of customs and a certain way of living, but I know Isa Masih died and lived again and, because of this, I know the heart of Khuda. I know His will if I ask it. He speaks to me.'

'You're a secret believer,' whispered Jasper, astounded at Sohail's strength of conviction. He wished he had the same faith.

'You may call me what you will. My parents know—my father is not radical in his beliefs as some are.'

'How did you hear about Isa?' Even though he didn't want to, Jasper felt the interest rise in him.

'I heard it from a man called Pembley Sahib—your father. It seems he did not tell you much!'

Jasper was suddenly miserable. 'No, he did tell me. When I was small, I knew it all; why I was, how God cares for each one of us. But when I got older ... well, when Dad died—'

It was as if Sohail knew what he was thinking, and he cut in, even angrier than before. 'You are a fool! A hundred camels should kick you! You had everything, yet you gave it up for this feeling of self-pity? It is the jinns that bring such thoughts as these. So, you are angry with Khuda because he took something precious away. He is the creator of everything.' He stood and spread his arms, then pointed back at Jasper. 'Do you not think he has a right to take away anything he wishes and have good reason for doing so? Who are you—a mosquito—that you argue with the ruler of the stars and planets?'

Jasper watched him in growing horror. No one had ever spoken to him like this. Everyone at school had known he was grieving and had treated him with kid gloves, giving him time to work through it. Yet, he had let the feelings fester and grow into what had become a cancer. Slowly he began to see himself in a different light, and it wasn't pretty. Sohail was right: he was angry. He hated even the idea of God. He had let his dad die, and there hadn't even been a funeral. Always the regret that he should have been there, and wasn't.

Then he couldn't help it: sobs jumped out like the breaths of a drowned man given mouth-to-mouth. He hadn't cried before, not for his dad. For the first time, he realised there was nothing he could have done, and he was so sorry. Sorry that he had turned his back on all that his father had lived for and believed in; sorry that in an attempt to make everything right again, he'd almost caused the girls' deaths. Jasper never noticed Sohail leave, but as he glanced around, he realised he was alone in the night. Yet, he felt less alone than he had since word had first come about his dad's disappearance.

Sohail returned, their turbans in his hand and Jasper

stood facing him in the moon's light. Slowly, Jasper held out his hand. The young Pakhtun smiled and stepped forward to embrace him in a hug.

'Now I see we are truly brothers. The peace of Khuda is in you.'

Jasper nodded and heaved a shuddering sigh.

Sohail took his arm. 'Now we must go, and quickly. A party of men are out from the fort. We have to get the girls to safety. Sonya must not go back to the village but now it is too dangerous on the road. I know a place. Raza!'

22

Jasper

Sohail had left his horse tethered over the other side of the gully and as he and Jasper skidded up to it, he pulled his Kalashnikov from the saddle, threw himself down and lay as if in an ambush behind a fallen log. Jasper dropped down beside him.

'Sorry I have no gun for you, my friend.' Sohail had sounded especially concerned about that, but Jasper wasn't used to guns, certainly not automatic assault rifles.

Soon they saw the dark shapes coming up over the ridge, the guns and turbans silhouetted against the night sky behind them.

'Are they guerrillas?'

'Ji,' Sohail's voice was tense and strangely sad too. 'They call themselves mujahideen—fighters for freedom like my people—except these ones are terrorists only. They say Islam calls for violence to make our country an Islamic state, but this is not the Islam my father follows. It is a pity they fight and kill innocent people—there are more important things in our country to do.' He let loose the safety-catch on the AK 47.

'Isn't there a better way than fighting back? Someone

could get killed.'

Sohail must have heard the desperate note in Jasper's voice—or did he recognise the fear? 'Not with these people, my friend,' he said. 'They understand no other way. There is no time to get the girls to safety—the men are too close. We must fight.'

Jasper could feel the sweat on his lip as he saw Sohail's finger tremble on the trigger. They both jumped involuntarily as a stream of slugs from a machine gun ripped a line of holes across the log. The horse shied and whinnied as Sohail's AK 47 rattled in return fire. Jasper ducked, nervous, as a tracer sang past his ear. One of the shots tore a harmless path through his coat sleeve and he wondered if they should change their position. He watched Sohail changing the magazine. In the lull, a voice boomed from the darkness in guttural Pakhtu.

'Surrender. We know you are but a boy. You have no hope.'

'Nay!' Sohail shouted and underlined his answer with a barrage of bullets.

The resulting cry of pain brought a satisfied mutter from Sohail. The guys squinted into the clearing ahead of them. The bright flashes drew closer and there were many pockets of darkness to serve as hiding places. Jasper couldn't imagine how Sohail would keep the whole group at bay, especially when he'd wounded only one.

Just then, their hiding place was shredded by a storm of bullets from the side. Jasper grunted as he was flung backwards. Something slammed into his shoulder like a fourth of July rocket. He gingerly touched his arm and found it wet and sticky.

'Sohail, I'm hit. They're closing in. If you get shot too, what will happen to the girls? They can't hope to escape. We have to surrender. It would be different if it were only us, but we must protect them. Sohail! Are you listening?'

'You do not understand,' Sohail growled. 'We never give up.'

Jasper did understand. He knew the code of honour of Pakhtuns, but he also knew that the girls would be hopeless without help. There was no doubt the men would find them. What did Sohail think the two of them could do? For once, Jasper wanted to make the right decision.

It was over in a matter of minutes. Sohail shouted in Pakhtu and threw his rifle into the darkness. As he pulled Jasper up beside him, the men from the fort urged their mounts nearer. It was obvious, even in the pale light, that they recognised Sohail and were surprised to see him there.

'So, a prize!' A huge burly man with ammunition straddling his chest dismounted and moved so close to the boys that Jasper could smell the garlic on his breath. 'My father will be pleased to see you, son of the khan.' He spat the last word out as though there was no such title, and laughed like a jackal, the men with him echoing the evil sound.

At that moment, Jasper knew Sohail had been right; falling alive into the hands of men like these was a terrible mistake. Mr Kumar had been a mujahid and so was Sohail. Stupidly, he'd thought all militants would be like them, keeping the Pakhtunwali, the ancient code of honour.

23

Jaime

It wasn't long before Liana was bending over and groaning. She had no time to explain, and with sharp signals that she needed a bush, she hurried out of sight. I hoped she'd be better soon. That was when I thought I could hear banging like fireworks. It was hard to distinguish one sound from another in the wind near the waterfall. I moved down a little and then I heard another noise: shouts and what sounded like gunfire.

Something was wrong. From where Sonya and I were, I couldn't hear much except the firing, then came a lull. After that, the snort of a horse, close by. I was so relieved they'd returned that I forgot Jasper's instruction to stay hidden until I heard his voice, and rushed out to meet them. I even had the veil of the burqa flung back.

Sonya tried to hold my horse by the bridle, but it didn't stop me. The bawdy shouts and whoops that met me as I emerged from behind the cover did though. The men didn't seem surprised we were there, just obscenely pleased that they'd found us—with a lot of help from me, I was horrified to realise. I expected Sonya to tell me what she thought of me, but she was silent. At least Liana was safely hidden behind a bush.

When we were led into the circle of militants and forced off our mounts so that two men without horses could ride, I felt as if I'd been told to swim across a shark-infested estuary. Life to that point had just been a practice; this was the reality. Men like these would behead the boys without thinking about it and make us girls their war wives. Life and death hung in the balance, and I didn't like the odds. I could tell Jasper didn't either. He stood crookedly, looking dazed. He couldn't even hold himself up. Sohail was studying Sonya and me in our burqas, as if he had Superman's x-ray vision and didn't like what he saw.

Suddenly, Sohail spoke to the largest of the men. He sounded arrogant, just like the day he warned us by emptying the magazine in the valley. Yet, this time I knew it was aggression born of fear. From the men's glances at us, I could tell he was talking about us. Probably warning them that we were his sisters. No doubt saving our virtue would be more important to Sohail than telling the truth. But from the sneers in the men's voices, I knew they wouldn't take notice of Sohail.

We were forced to walk then. Afghanistan can be a rocky place and that night, I felt we'd found the most barren part of all. Even the moon didn't help. I'd heard stories of freedom fighters covering forty kilometres a day; they had a rolling way of walking that enabled them to handle the rocky terrain, but I just kept tripping. Walking in a long burqa was so confining. How did the women here cope with wearing them all the time? I tried to keep close to Jasper; I didn't want any of those cutthroats getting near me, and besides, he was stumbling even more than I was.

Sohail fell back in step beside him and I overheard his strange query. 'Can you hold on a little longer, my friend?'

Jasper must have nodded for I heard nothing again, except his harsh breathing until he asked, 'Sohail?'

'Ji?'

He continued in Urdu. 'Why did you say you were betrothed to one of the girls? Just to save them?'

'Nay, because it is true,' came the simple answer. 'It is not yet made known.'

'You can't mean Jaime or Liana?'

Sohail hesitated only a second. 'My brother, you still have much to learn. Your sisters are my sisters, just as they are yours.' I didn't miss the inflection in Sohail's voice. Jasper must have caught it as well, for he made a small questioning sound.

'Ji, I know they are not your blood relatives. Pembley Sahib never spoke of his daughters. Also I know they are Australian.'

'Why did you allow the pretence ... I mean, if you knew?'

'I understood their honour was important to you. It did not need to be forbidden. But do not be concerned, only my father and I know this.'

'Then, who?'

Yes, I, too, was dying to know who he could possibly be engaged to.

'My betrothed is Sonya.'

I heard the bewilderment in Jasper's voice echoing that in my own mind. 'I never saw you pay her any attention.'

'That is not our custom. It would have been most unseemly and disrespectful to her to do so.'

'But you talked to Jaime.'

'That is different. Jaime could not be my wife. She is as a sister.'

Jasper was quiet after that; it was enough to keep me thinking for hours. Sonya! I wondered if she knew. Maybe that would explain how her behaviour changed in the village. It was too difficult to think through, especially when I was in danger of crippling myself on the rocks while we were herded up the steep hillside.

Liana was on my mind all the way up the mountain, hoping she would find Sonya's mare and return to the village. We'd just spent a lot of trouble getting out of there, thinking we were in danger, but in comparison to these men, Mr Kumar was as benign as Uncle Jon. Mr Kumar was a commander, surely he would organise help if he knew. I prayed Liana was well enough, that she'd manage to tell Mr Kumar and he would believe her.

I was cold and it felt as if we'd been walking half the night when I looked up and saw dark walls silhouetted against the night sky. It seemed like two! Then I brushed my eyes and focused again; it was the long wall of the fort that we'd seen from the van when we first arrived. We approached a giant wooden gate. The carving on it looked as though it had been crafted hundreds of years ago. It opened slowly like a monster yawning, and I had the uneasy thought that once we walked through, there would be no way out.

Inside lay a typical mountain village, and we were pushed down a narrow bazaar lane, the horses' hooves making clip-clopping sounds on the ancient worn stonework. A tower-like structure, which resembled an Afghan version of The Adams Family set, loomed in front of us. I had a strange floating sensation that I might as well be dead. Everyone back home most probably thought I was.

By that time, I knew there was something desperately wrong with Jasper. Sohail was supporting him as they walked down the lane. I'd been concentrating so hard on getting up the rocky ridge without spraining an ankle that I hadn't noticed how long Sohail had been helping him. When we stopped at the foot of the tower, it was as though Jasper knew he didn't have to make the effort any more, for he collapsed on to the ground. Even Sohail couldn't hold him.

I stood there staring at his body and didn't feel a thing. Through the haze of exhaustion I could have been watching a movie in a theatre, sight and sound echoing from behind the curtains. Soon someone would flick a switch, the lights would come on and I'd be safe at home.

24

Jaime

We were taken first of all to another man, obviously the commander—newspapers back home would have called him a war lord or a terrorist. He was already angry from being woken from his sleep. With him was a guard-type person who stared at us with the vacancy of a lunatic, except when the war lord gave him an order. Then, the man's eyes took on the fire of a fanatic. My numbness as Jasper fell and was dragged away began to recede and in its place there grew a crawling horror. What would they do to him? So much for the theory of our minds letting us stay in suspended shock at traumatic moments.

There, in the war lord's room, I heard the threat in the man's tone as he spoke and towered over us; I watched his lopsided leer widen as his curved knife came close to Sohail's neck and drew blood from the finest of cuts. Sohail didn't flinch as his eyes blazed back into his tormentor's. At that moment, I felt I'd been right about one thing at least—Sohail was noble, regardless of what Jasper thought. I'd never forget the way he looked right then, like a prince standing in a circle of thieves, knowing they would kill him, but keeping his courage and dignity to the end.

The war lord leaned in closer, almost like a friend, and spoke in Pakhtu to Sohail. Sonya took in a sudden breath beside me and I wished I knew what he'd said.

The men's attention quickly turned to Sonya and me. The laughter as our burqas were ripped off was obscene, and that was when Sohail acted. He lunged forward, but two men from the corridor rushed in and held him. One grabbed him under his neck so he couldn't breathe without turning his face to the ceiling. It was hard to tell what amused the war lord the most—playing with Sonya's and my fears, or watching Sohail lose his cool.

There was no doubt what would happen to us and I was glad Liana was safe.

The man stepped towards Sonya and me then. 'So, one of you is Ruse, the other Inglestan.' Then came the words in broken English, 'Such beauty. More than the telling.' He laughed, lust making his eyes shine.

He leaned near to my ear; I recoiled from his evil-smelling breath and the matted remains of dinner on his black beard. 'How entertaining it will be deciding which is which.' He lifted up a piece of my hair with his knife and flicked it slightly. I stared, mesmerised as two centimetres of my hair floated to the floor. I couldn't stop shivering as his laugh filled the room.

Then his attention was drawn to a scuffle outside the door. I breathed in at the reprieve. But it was short-lived. A man threw in a burqa-clad woman so that she landed on the floor at the war lord's feet. His barked words sounded like an accusation.

The war lord still had the knife in one hand as he pulled the woman to her feet. A new, deeper fear gripped me. The woman was the same height as Liana. Surely not. He flicked up the burqa with the knife to show a pale-faced Liana, her dark hair over one cheek, eyes tightly shut. 'So, another one.' He spoke in Urdu this time. 'Why were you out in the night alone? To tell secrets?'

Liana's eyes flew open as she shook her head, but she showed no fear other than the widening of her pupils.

'Nay, there is only one reason a woman is out in the dark and that is to meet with men and give herself to them. This is immoral behaviour and needs to be purged, so we can have a pure land. You will be whipped.'

I gasped and before I could stop myself, I spoke. 'It's not true. She is pure, we all are pure.'

The war lord laughed. 'How can I believe that? You were in the dark with two young men who are not your husbands. This evil behaviour cannot go unpunished or we will have an immoral nation like the West. We are fighting for a pure Islamic state and people like you need to be made an example of.' He barked an order to the vacant-eyed guard, no doubt to take us away.

The war lord's insane laughing followed us out of the room. Our hope of rescue was gone.

ا‌ل‌ه

It was the early hours of the morning when we were dragged into the tower of the fort and thrown into a room. At least we'd all been imprisoned together. It was unusual but maybe they could spare only one guard. Vacant Eyes gave an order to Sohail then shut the door behind him. Sohail translated when he left. 'We have to behave ourselves or he'll be in here to beat us.'

The first thing I did was hug Liana and garbled out my concerns. 'Are you well now? I'm sad you were found, I was hoping—'

She cut in, 'I think the shock has fixed my sickness. I heard what happened to you, even found the horse, and was on my way to get help. But they must have left a few men to check the area. I'm sorry.' There was nothing more to say.

It was a relief to see Jasper lying on the only charpai. He was unconscious. Blood oozed down his arm and dripped onto the floor. I knelt by the bed to touch his forehead. He moved slightly and moaned. The sound encouraged me, and I checked under his vest. It seemed he was only wounded in the shoulder. I hesitated before doing what I did next. It wasn't easy—I loved that tribal dress—but I couldn't let Jasper bleed to death. I ripped off a piece of the material from the hem and wrapped it around the top part of his arm. Soon, I was wishing I knew some first aid, as it wasn't long before the cloth was looking darker, glistening in the early light of the morning.

He didn't wake, so I sat on the stone floor next to the charpai. I surveyed the grimy, colourless room we'd been thrown into. It was bare except for the string bed and a clay water jar. Only a bucket stood closed off in a corner. How embarrassing it would be to relieve ourselves, or were we only to be here for a short time before they 'punished' us? The walls of our prison were cobwebbed and the dusty floor crawled with scuttling cockroaches. Worse, every time

I moved or scratched myself, I saw tiny black things jump. Even the air smelt musty. And it was cold. They sure didn't roll out the red carpet.

Sohail, panther-like, paced the room. It was nerve-wracking to watch him. Sonya was a mess. All the things I'd thought about her when we first met—that she was weird but brave, bossy but occasionally kind—melted away like ice in a fire. She just sat there, rocking herself. I moved closer and put an arm around her. It was the first time I'd been that close without her pulling away.

'I'm sure we'll be all right. Maybe Sohail's father will realise we are gone, send out a party of men.' The words sounded empty, even to me. I'd never been big on telling lies. The look on her face would have stopped me from saying more anyway.

'No.' Sonya gulped down a sob. 'Mujahideen are supposed to be fighting jihad or holy war but these people are terrorists fighting for power and using Islam as a screen. They are the sort of men who block the aid, and sell information and behead people if they do not do what they want. They deal in hashish to get arms and do not care which country they give information to. Men like this killed my mother and—and we shall never get out of here alive.'

Tears filled her eyes and I couldn't understand how she went through so many emotional fluctuations. We were kidnapped in the village, yet she was fine then.

Liana spoke, maybe to lighten Sonya's mood, or to keep our minds off the horror. 'I've been impressed how you've taken everything in your stride. You were so brave in Peshawar and calm in the village.'

Sonya turned to face us, and I was shocked at the

hopelessness in her face. 'That was because I knew. Do you not see? When Sohail captured us, I realised who he was. I saw a family likeness. Uncle Kumar—'

'He's your real uncle?' Talk about true confessions.

'Yes, and Sohail is my cousin. We were never in any danger.' She gulped a breath. 'I wanted to help. I wanted to see Afghanistan unified, rebuilt and strong again, not like a strict Islamic state. But a place where girls can study, women are allowed to work, and the poor and sick are cared for. Many people do their part in some way. It is always risky, and many do not understand the tangle of intrigue that is woven between foreign nations and all the different parties that want to rule. So many Afghans care little for that kind of unity when they fight in the mountains far from Kabul.'

'So Jasper was wrong, you are not working for a Western country.'

'No, I found out information—like which country was giving arms to which party, and how much—and I would tell Uncle Kumar. I think some countries, especially the superpowers, say they are helping but they only send enough arms to keep the mujahideen and the government fighting, never enough to let them win and unite the country. And without this unity we will destroy ourselves. My father never knew what I did. I had made a mistake, a political agent must have followed me, just before you came. I was very worried and I am sorry I took it out on you. That was when Uncle Kumar thought of the idea of kidnapping me to make it seem I was not helping him.'

'But it all went wrong.'

'Yes.'

'Why didn't you let us go in Peshawar?'

'It was too dangerous. You were followed from the capital by an agent also, but we were not sure if he was Russian or Pakistani.'

'Pakistani?'

'Many do not want Afghanistan to unite, to have the freedom that the West believe was won for us after September 11. Also, my uncle's honour was at stake. It was our fault you were involved in this. We were honour-bound to mend it. When my uncle realised that Jasper was the son of his old friend, he had double resolve to keep all of you safe.'

She paused, then said, 'My father will be waiting for me. That was our plan. I managed to meet him one night at the village.'

So much for Jasper's idea of her meeting with an agent. 'That's why you left your mare and were on foot at the rendezvous?'

She tilted her head. 'Now he will not know where I am. It is dangerous for him too.'

'Why?'

'He is Russian. There is always talk that there is a move to gather the Asian states together again. Some Afghans would like them to be part of Afghanistan, and people have not forgotten that Russia has lost her path to a warm port.'

There was more she said but I didn't understand the politics. By the time she had finished, I felt like any new aid worker who had worked in Afghanistan: that there was no way of piecing it all together. I simply said how sorry I was, and surprisingly, Sonya took my hand.

'I thought you and Liana were very brave—no, truly,

when you did not know what I knew. We could not tell you, in case the wrong people contacted you. It was to keep me safe, and now I am very sorry that in keeping me safe, you have come to harm.' The tears glistened in her eyes and I put my arm around her again. 'We shall die,' she said softly, 'but at least I have died for my country. I am sorry that you cannot say the same.'

I looked up to find Sohail's gaze on me. Some Afghans have an uncanny way of staring at you, but Sohail's was not like the vacant staring of the guard. It was communing—maybe he was telling me he was sorry, but he also looked resigned.

It disappointed me. Sohail had seemed different, and even though we'd never had deep conversations because of the cultural taboos, I thought we'd be kindred spirits in another culture and place. I'd never considered him as a person who'd sit and wait as if everything had been willed by God. It goaded me to ask him a question.

'Why did you say your village has nothing to do with this fort? Is it because they belong to a different political party or ethnic group?'

Sohail sighed and I wondered if such a question would take too long to answer. How much time did we have? I was about to tell him not to worry when he sat against the wall and spoke.

'It is an old story, and not a pretty one. We were related by blood to the people from the fort. There was a feud, you understand?'

I nodded.

'It all started with my aunt. She was very beautiful. She studied in Kabul and was able to work in a government office for a while. Educated women could do those things in Kabul then, although strict imams were not happy about it. There was a Russian, an advisor to the government, working there also, and he wished to marry her. My maternal grandparents disagreed, saying it was an unsuitable arrangement. They were living in the village, in the fort at the time. My father's parents are the less conservative side of the family and agreed to the match. The groom even studied Islam to appease our angry relatives.' He paused a moment and I managed to stop myself asking what happened next.

'The couple never came here at first for fear of trouble, but one time they did. They had a beautiful little daughter. They thought that if they could only show her to her grandparents, there would be reconciliation. For what grandparents would not love their own blood?' Pain flared in his eyes. 'My aunt was killed by an extremist young fool who understood nothing. My aunt's Russian husband has been only half a man since, immersing himself in his work, not knowing how to properly bring up his daughter. We have become her family instead.'

I quietly said, 'The baby is Sonya.'

Sohail glanced at Sonya and tipped his head to the side. He didn't say any more.

Liana whispered to me, 'God will help us, we only have to ask Him.' She squeezed my hand.

I prayed as I touched Jasper's forehead again, noticing his hair was darker from the sweat of fever. He felt so hot, yet I was freezing and finding it hard to keep awake. I knew it wasn't a good idea to sleep, but I was exhausted. How many kilometres did we walk across the Afghan mountains? It felt like a hundred.

The last thing I remember seeing was the baleful stare of the guard watching us from the grimy window in the door.

25

Jaime

A noise woke me and my eyes flew open. It still wasn't morning as far as I could tell.

'Dad!' Jasper called out as he rolled onto his shoulder.

I crawled over to the bed. 'Jasper? Are you okay?' What a dumb thing to say, but my mind was foggy. He didn't even open his eyes.

'Mum? I fell ... off the bike. I hurt so bad.' Then he shouted, 'Where's Dad?'

Sohail moved closer.

'He's delirious,' Liana said and I hoped Sohail would know what to do.

Then I said, 'Jas, it's okay. It's me, Jaime.' I rested my hand on his head again; he was burning up. He groaned and I brushed my arm across my face, not entirely to scrape hair from my eyes. I was still blinking when I poured water out of the clay pot onto another piece of my dress to wipe his face.

Sohail watched me for a moment, then felt Jasper's head himself. When he spoke, I heard an echo of the misery I felt, and the fatigue. 'I have seen this before. Men would be brought to the village from the fighting with bullet wounds. If they got fevers, they died, unless a doctor was found.'

'He won't die!' I felt stupid for saying it: we were all going to die.

There was a big-brotherly type of compassion in Sohail's face. It almost made me cry properly, so I looked at Jasper instead. Tears fell onto Jasper's face. He didn't flinch and I knew then I'd do all I could for him. I understood that grief for his father had eaten him up and made him moody, trying to prove himself; that it'd been difficult for him being where his father had been killed. But he was still Jasper. We'd shared too much at school since we were six, and I cared.

'Would there be a doctor here?' I asked Sohail.

'We shall have to send for a hakim. They should have one.' Sohail called for the guard.

'Not a hakim!' I couldn't imagine the fort having a trained healer. 'That won't help him now—just some old remedy. He needs the bullet taken out.'

'There is no other way,' Sohail returned gently, but I didn't miss the firmness in his voice, nor the pain. It was as though he truly cared. How could that have happened when all Jasper had shown him was anger and sarcasm? The thought distracted me a moment until Vacant Eyes unlocked the door and looked in, frowning.

He took one glance at Jasper, growled and stood over the bed. He must have been told to hold our lives lightly because he whisked out a knife like the war lord's and with his other hand, ripped open Jasper's shirt. It all happened so fast. The buttons popped, Jasper moaned before I could even scream a protest. All I could do was stare, watching the knife descend.

Then suddenly, Vacant Eyes made a peculiar sound. He abruptly sheathed the knife and, with a lingering look at Jasper but not a glance at the rest of us, he left the room. Sohail, poised like a cat, suddenly flopped on to the floor. So did I.

'Now what's going on?' I murmured. No one answered. Seeing Jasper nearly killed made me realise afresh what the future held and how naïve I'd been to think it could be any different.

ﷺ

In the morning I was woken by Jasper calling my name. 'Jaime. Is there any water?'

It was a special moment. 'Jas! You sound so much better.' The bandages were a surprise too. 'When did that happen?'

'No idea. It seems a hakim has been here, though.'

I took the clay pot over to him. 'This will be full of amoeba.'

'Amoeba are the least of our problems right now.' His eyes glazed over as he tried to raise himself and fell back on the bed.

Sohail rushed to his side to lift him.

'I'll hold your head up, Jasper,' I said. 'Just sip.'

As the pain subsided, his eyes cleared again and his gaze rested on Sonya. Realisation dawned on his face and he winced as he tried to move again. 'Sohail. You knew it was Sonya last night, didn't you?'

The young Pakhtun gave a slight smile as he inclined his head. 'Burqas do not hide the way a girl walks or holds her head.'

'Then where's Liana?'

I sighed as I set down the water jar. Liana came forward so Jasper could see her. 'When we were ambushed last night, or this morning, I wasn't well. I was in the bushes and heard everything. I was returning to the village—'

'When they caught you too,' Jasper said tiredly.

'How bad do you think it is, Jas?' I said. Do you think they'll let us go? For money? Are we hostages?'

He was quiet for such a long time that I thought he must have dropped off to sleep, when he slowly answered. 'I'm not sure. I thought we were hostages in the village and had to get out, but I was wrong. I'm sorry.' He had a kind of 'I don't deserve you to like me' look on his face. I squeezed his hand. Anything negative I felt about him disappeared when I'd wiped his face with strips of my tribal dress. He must have been in the mood for confessions because he continued.

'You know Mr Kumar told me how Dad died. I haven't handled it all very well, right from the start. But I feel I can face it now. All that fear and anger because I wasn't there for Dad—maybe I'll still have problems with it, but I don't feel like it's controlling me any more. Now I reckon I could get to breaking point and I wouldn't flip all over the place like I was. Sohail told me a few things too.'

Jasper told me all that had happened the night before with Sohail. I was sure the others could hear him as well. 'Actually it was more like a camel kick up the backside. Sohail's counselling methods wouldn't go down well in the West. Jaime?' He reached up, touching my face just like he had when he went scouting the night before, and wiped away the tear rolling down my cheek. 'You're crying.'

'It's just that ever since I came back here, I've been so worried about you. I wanted us to be friends again, like we were before I left to go to Australia. I know you still cared or you wouldn't have tried to get us out of the village, but it wasn't the same.'

'No.' Then I felt Jasper's good hand on my neck drawing me down. I didn't think to resist or even wonder if the others were watching. His kiss was gentle, gentler than I would have thought, and for a moment, I forgot about forts and assault rifles and wars. I sat up, still holding his hand.

'Friends again?' His eyes were smiling like they used to.

'Yeah. Why did you kiss me?'

'I wanted to do that all through Year 10 and I kicked myself after you'd gone. I'd never told you just how much you meant and I don't want that to happen again. If we get out of here, or if we don't, I want you to know how special you are.'

'Thanks, Jas.' Then I grinned. 'Remember how we used to compare scratches and scabs to see who had the biggest?' He nodded, grinning too as I gently touched his bandages. 'Guess you win again.'

Jasper's bandages were an encouraging sign. Why would they have bothered fixing him if killing us was the next item on their agenda? I tried to get Sonya to see the logic of that, but she wouldn't be consoled. Sohail kept tight-lipped too. I guess he knew about these people; I didn't.

One interesting thing happened, though. It seemed Jasper was suddenly on their list of special guests. Mid-morning, Vacant Eyes came in with breakfast—on a tray. Even the naan was warm. It reminded me a bit of the morning Sohail brought breakfast to us in Peshawar, but try as I might, I could not transform Vacant Eyes into Sohail's dashing figure. Unfortunately, the breakfast this time was only for Jasper, and Vacant Eyes stood there, making sure Jasper was the only one who ate it.

'Go on, Jas. You need it anyway.' Besides, I reckoned the guard would let us finish off what Jasper didn't eat. That must have been in Jasper's mind too, for he soon finished, and the guard simply looked annoyed when Jasper handed us the rest. It was as if he wouldn't stop anything Jasper wanted to do. I had the unpleasant thought that if we'd put our hands out to take it, our fingers would have been sliced off.

After Vacant Eyes disappeared from the room in a huff, leaving us to finish the breakfast, I said, 'Why are they treating you like a prince?'

No one answered.

26

Jaime

Sohail was busy studying the mud walls. 'These are hundreds of years old,' he murmured to nobody in particular. He'd taken to talking in Urdu or English—so we'd all understand, I guess. Then he stood up and started his pacing again. I was struggling to not let what I privately called his panther prance unnerve me, when I saw his foot catch on a rough part of the floor. I expected his sharp exclamation in Pakhtu, but not the hype that was suddenly in his tone.

'Raza! Come!' he urged. Even Sonya crawled over with Liana and me. All we could see was a square piece of wood set into the mud floor. Sohail had dragged back the canvas-like stuff covering the floor and was scraping years of dirt and mildew to one side.

'What is it?' Sonya asked.

Sohail tried prising up the wood with his fingers. It wasn't moving and his breath came in puffs. I gave him the spoon from the tray to use as a lever and crouched down to help him; so did Sonya. Finally we lifted up a giant spider's trapdoor. I stared down into the dark cavity below.

'Do you know what I think it is?' I actually clutched Sohail's arm. 'Once we went to Rohtas Fort near Jhelum and there was a whole underground well system. One of the Moghul emperors had it built. There were passages that even went outside the fort walls. Sohail! We could escape!'

He stared back at me steadily, as if refusing to share my level of excitement. 'What if it is not?'

Jasper's voice came from the bed. 'I vote we try it and see where it leads. If we tried at night, it mightn't matter if we have to come back.'

'That guard listens to everything,' Sonya said. 'He was in here like a gunshot when Jasper was ill.'

'I shall take care of him.' And Sohail smacked his fist into his hand.

I grinned at him. I knew he would rally. But my elation died as I watched him stand and move to the window, his head cocked to one side.

'We may not be able to wait for tonight. Sunno!'

I heard the sound of a mullah on the loudspeaker from the mosque, his voice fanatical, rising in a crescendo to a screech at the end of every few sentences.

'The mullahs in villages like this are masters at inciting the people,' he said.

It sounded ominous in the sudden quiet of our dingy quarters and I could barely hear my own voice as I asked, 'What's he saying?'

'Kill the infidels, kill Kumar's son and purify the village of evil. Allah will be pleased with such devotion … He will bless this jihad …' Then Sohail stopped, listening again. 'There are other matters like that,' was all he said then. I knew there was more he didn't want to say. I looked over at Jasper. He was watching me, his mouth tightened.

'How's your arm feel, Jas?' I went over to check and lifted the blanket that had been wrapped around him. I didn't know what to look for but at least no blood was showing through the bandages. Then I stopped in surprise.

'Jas! I thought the only jewellery you wore was your mum's cross.'

He fingered it where it lay in the gap where his shirt was half off. 'She let me wear it because I missed Dad so much. They'd had identical ones. Some teenage exchange they did years ago.'

I winked at him. 'Then where did you get the wedding ring, Jas?' It was strange I hadn't noticed it before.

'Wedding ring?' His surprise was convincing. He looked at his hands, and there it was, on his injured one. It was obvious he hadn't put it on himself.

'I don't know.' He took it off and rubbed it, turning it over. He glanced on the inside and drew in a quick breath.

'What is it?' I was straining to see, and soundlessly he handed it over. I read the inscription inside: *Joe, love Marie.* I looked at him, eyebrows up. 'So?'

'It's my father's wedding ring,' he said flatly. 'One of the men here must have found it. I don't think I can stand it—a guy wearing Dad's ring all this time.'

I should have heeded the desolate tone in his voice but I was too excited by the possibilities. 'Don't you think it would be a good idea to meet the person? It must have been someone who came with the hakim, if not the hakim himself. I wonder why he would do it?'

'Thought I'd die, I suppose.'

'Or knew you were Western, and thought you might like it. They'd know the words were English maybe.'

'Jaime, stop it! I can't see the hakim. What would I ask? Oh, where did you find my father's finger? Were there any other parts of his body lying around? Did you think to bury them?' The old sarcasm and anger in his voice shocked me into silence, but only for a moment.

'Jas, I'm sorry, I wasn't thinking.' But the ring had started a wild hope in my heart. 'Just think, Jas. Whoever did that must be friendly. And we need a friend in this place. We might be able to bribe him to help us.'

Sohail watched us both. Then he spoke. It was the only time he ever interfered in a conversation between Jasper and myself. 'She is right, my friend.'

Jasper kept silent. I could tell he was wrestling with his emotions, but I knew how difficult it is to fight feelings with more feelings.

'Jas? You know something changed for you the other night. Just hang on to that, whether you feel it or not.'

Sohail said as if quoting a poem,

'Let me forget the war and cruelty inside myself …

Only you can restore what You have broken;

help my broken head. I'm not asking for sweet pistachio candy,

but Your everlasting love.'

'That's beautiful,' I said. 'Did you write it?'

He smiled with his hand over his heart. 'Nay, this is from our famous poet, Rumi.'

Jasper sighed heavily, as though blowing away his negative thoughts and found it hard work. 'Okay. How do you think we could get the hakim back in?'

It was Liana who had the idea. 'Act sick. You could call for the guard, Sohail?'

Sohail seemed only too pleased to have some plan of action. Sonya was at my elbow as I dripped water over Jasper to make him look sweaty.

'What if it doesn't work?' she asked. 'What if they do not truly care about Jasper and kill him?'

Jasper answered her. 'We have to try.'

Then Sohail called to the guard to bring the hakim quickly. Vacant Eyes took one look through the dirty window at Jasper tossing and moaning on the bed and promptly disappeared. It looked as if they wanted Jasper alive, after all.

Sohail gave me the international thumbs up and I grinned. Afghans seem to thrive on action and danger; Sohail was almost glowing. The door opened then and Jasper kept the act up in case the guard came in too. Sohail's job was to divert him, but just then a guttural voice from the ground barked out an order and Vacant Eyes quickly locked the door and left.

What happened then was another frozen-in-time moment when you can remember everything: people's expressions, how they stood, what they said. Sohail's mouth dropped open when he turned and saw who had come in the door. Liana and I watched, equally astounded. Sonya must have wondered why we looked so shell-shocked.

The man set down his bag and leaned over the bed where Jasper had his eyes shut, still moaning. The man felt Jasper's vital points, and spoke at the same time. 'Son, I thought you'd be all right.' No one could have mistaken the anguish in that voice.

Sonya was glancing around, bewildered, just as Jasper instantly grew rigid on the bed. His eyes flew open, the disbelief in them making him seem crazed. For some seconds no one spoke.

'Are you real?' Jasper finally whispered. 'Not a hallucination?'

'Not a hallucination.' The man smiled, and bit his lip the way I've seen Dad do to keep his face from folding up.

Suddenly Jasper flung himself into the arms of the older man. 'I thought you were dead. They told me your van had hit a mine.'

How could I describe what that moment was like? Sonya began to catch on because her eyes watered like mine and Liana's. Sohail's whole stance was that of a man standing for a master.

After a while, Jasper let himself be lowered onto the bed. 'I'd just got used to it. And finally when I accepted that you'd gone, I got you back.'

He laughed, but it was the hysterical laugh of the overwrought, and Joe Pembley glanced quickly at the door.

'Son, you'll need to quieten down. I'm a prisoner here, like you, and the only reason I'm alive is because I'm a doctor. These fighters will never kill a doctor.'

'How did you escape the landmine? Or was that only a lie to keep me quiet?'

'There was a bomb blast—the van I was travelling in swerved off the road. I fell out. Then it did hit a mine. That's why you would have been told I was dead. Parts of the van were found. I was wounded, unconscious, and militants from the fort found me. I've been here ever since. This place is a fortress. No one else knows I'm here, and it's impossible to escape.'

'So why do they want me alive?'

'The guard saw the cross. He's seen mine. He's not educated, so, in his logic, if one man has a thing around his neck and he's a doctor, and another man has the same thing around his neck, he's a doctor too. Welcome to the fraternity, son.'

Dr Pembley looked around at all of us then. Introductions were made for Sonya. He remembered me and Liana from school functions. And when he clasped Sohail in a hug, it was obvious there was a special bond between them.

'The doctor work is elementary here.' Dr Pembley was talking to Jasper again. 'Cutting out bullets, stitching, bandaging. I could teach you. It'll be the only way you will survive.' He turned to Sohail then, and said, 'Sorry' so softly, but I caught it. I knew why he said it — for Sohail there was no such hope.

Sohail spoke then. 'The girls?'

Jasper's father didn't answer straight away, but he looked steadily at Sohail for some moments before he did. 'They won't kill them, not yet.' Sohail shuddered—from fear on our behalf, or anger, I couldn't tell. 'Not all the men here are crazy,' Mr Pembley added. 'Some were forced to join to save their families. We can pray the girls are treated kindly.'

'We have a plan, Dad. It mightn't work, but at least we could try. Jaime thinks there might be an underground passage leading to a well and maybe to the outside. Like at Rohtas Fort.'

Dr Pembley considered it. 'Yeah, I suppose it is possible. Many old forts had a well system built into them in the beginning so they'd be safe during a siege. They've been forgotten about now, I should think.'

'That's what we're counting on, Dr Pembley,' I broke in. 'If no one knows, then they won't think to look for us there.'

'Dad?' Jasper leaned forward. 'Can you get back in here, later on? Tonight—on pretence of checking me out again, and we'll try it? Sohail found what might be part of a passage.'

'I suppose so.' Dr Pembley ran his fingers through his thinning hair. 'Seeing you again gives me new hope. Perhaps it'll work, perhaps not, but anything will be better than sitting around watching what happens to you kids.'

In a few more minutes, Vacant Eyes arrived to take Jasper's father away. No doubt he was congratulating himself on finding another healer for he actually swaggered as if Jasper's recovery was all his doing.

We tried to plan what could happen if this or that eventuated. I was scared—only a fool wouldn't have been— but it was exciting too. Liana's eyes shone at the miracle of Mr Pembley's appearance. Sohail had the buoyed-up look of a leopard before a hunt; Jasper was itching to get on with it too. Even Sonya entered into the planning, her spirits reviving.

Sohail did give us one sobering thought. 'You realise that if we are caught doing this, it will be worse than if we did not. We will be punished twice over.'

None of us said anything, just stared at him until he smiled.

'Accha, it is good. Only I had to warn you. Now we are ready.'

27

Jaime

At the time of afternoon prayers, we were woken abruptly from our dozing by the door being dragged open. Since Jasper's breakfast, we'd had nothing else to eat and my head felt like a spinning blade on a helicopter. My little sister, Elly, would have complained of malnutrition long before. Jasper struggled to sit up when he saw his father coming through the door. Just before he reached Jasper's bed, he turned and spoke to Vacant Eyes. I don't know what he said but the guard promptly left and locked the door.

'How did you manage that, Dr Pembley?' I asked.

He smiled ruefully. 'It's not who you know, but whose life you've saved that matters in a place like this. That man tries to be grateful—most of the time. Now,' his tone became brisk, 'you must get yourselves together. Quickly. Here's a shirt for you, son, and put the vest on again. We can't wait for tonight. There's movement in the fort that doesn't include your wellbeing. Especially not Sohail's.'

He took out some Afghan sweets. 'Eat these. They'll raise your blood sugar, if nothing else.' I popped the sugar-coated almonds in my mouth. Dad used to buy me those when I was a kid. He called them 'nuckle'.

'Good.' Dr Pembley gave the smile of a doctor about to take blood. 'Now, where is this passage you think you've found?'

Sohail moved to the dimmest corner of the room and pulled up the trap door. We all stared into the black hole that yawned below us. I tried not to think what might be down there—spiders, snakes—just concentrated on the task ahead.

Outside, from the ground, we heard a burst of machine gun fire and Sohail stood up to face Dr Pembley. I could see the worried determination in the doctor's face and a weary sort of excitement in Sohail's.

'Now!' snapped Jasper's father. 'There's no time to lose. 'You first, Sohail, then the girls.' I could see where Jasper got his managing ways from, but just then, I didn't care. In times like that, someone always takes charge, and the people who do it best seem to know it's their role.

Jasper staggered off the string bed and his father moved to help him, but Jasper waved him off. 'Let's just get down there.'

Sohail had found footholds in the tunnel—old rods of wood that had been set into the mud and stone walls at half-metre intervals—and he directed Sonya and me on how to use them. I tried to squint past him but the shaft plunged into darkness. One false move could mean death, or at least a broken leg.

'Be careful,' came Sohail's whisper, the sound of it an eerie echo in the confined space of the shaft.

By the time Jasper managed with his good arm to drop down into the shaft, I could hear the chilling sound of a mob gone wild. Chanting voices were raised to a feverish shouting that gradually became a roar—'Allahu Akbar, God is great'—

as men called upon God to help them fight. I glanced up as Jasper found the first rung. Then I heard a new sound, like pounding on the walls of the fort. I hung on tighter to a rung. It felt as if the whole tower was shaking.

Dr Pembley pulled the trapdoor shut above him, and the noise from the ground lessened. 'Hope this looks normal when the guard comes back to get me. That is, if he's got time to come with all hell breaking loose out there.' No one answered. I felt like asking about the bagging that was on the floor; there would have been no way to hide the trapdoor again, but negotiating those rungs took up all my energy.

Finding each rung in that heavy blackness wasn't as easy as it sounded. The air was musty and stale, smelling five hundred years old, and those pieces of wood were so far apart. Each time I let go with one hand to reach down to the next, I was scared I'd miss or that they'd fall. If they were anything like the air I breathed in, they were probably rotten.

Just then, as I reached down, I felt something give slightly. I froze; the wood was loose. Then it broke away from the wall. I still had hold of the one above me, but I screamed as the dislodged rung came right away and fell past Sonya and Sohail. With an ugly thumping noise it thudded onto the bottom of the tunnel. At least there was a bottom, but I didn't have time to be thankful about that, dangling from one piece of wood that for all I knew might go the same way.

'What'll I do?'

Sohail's voice rose like a genie in a bottle. 'Find the crevice from where it came. Dig your fingers into it. Our people do not need pieces of wood to climb down mountains—nor do you.' I knew he only meant to urge me on, but really!

'You can do it, Jaime.' That was Jasper. 'Just pretend you're a goat and put two hands on the next rung down. Then you'll have stretching room to find the crevice.' Gradually, I began to breathe easier as I found another foothold, and felt dumb for panicking. Jasper was free with his advice for a person with only one good arm to use and I wondered how he was managing. Probably using his wounded arm more than he should be.

'It is not far now to the end,' Sohail called from the bottom of the shaft and soon we were all there with him, on level ground. Dr Pembley had a small torch and the dank and mouldy walls of the passage glistened in its light. Water must have seeped across the uneven floor because I felt, before I heard, the squelch when I walked.

'Ugh!' Sonya grabbed my arm at a scuttling sound. 'There must be rats.' I wished she hadn't said that.

'I think we're quite a few metres below ground level.' Dr Pembley helped us think of better things than which life forms shared the space with us.

'Now we have to find the well,' I prompted, eager to be out of that part of the tunnel. A sewer couldn't have smelt much worse.

'Single file then,' Dr Pembley suggested. 'You first again, Sohail.'

We all kept close to each other; even the thought of disappearing into a side passage in a place like that was terrifying. The floor steadily sloped downwards and, whenever we heard that scurrying sound, we moved closer together—for Sonya's sake, of course.

'Hie!' Sonya suddenly cried out as a rustling and squeaking thing flew at her head.

Jasper swung his good arm up to ward it off. 'It's okay—only a bat.'

'Only!' the poor girl shrieked. She moved in closer to Jasper as I fell back to walk behind them. I wondered if maybe he was sorry for all the things he'd said about Sonya. He didn't seem to mind her using him as a protective wall. The old Jasper in the village would have pushed her away.

Sohail called out from ahead. 'We have found the well!' He sounded as if he'd just taken the first steps on Mars. We milled around in awe. The ancient underground well stretched out before us, shining in the faint light from an open shaft fifty metres above us.

'It's huge,' I whispered. 'Like an underground swimming pool.'

The late afternoon sunlight filtered down, making little sparkles of radiance dance like fairies' wings on the still surface. Looking up, I could see tiny, fluffy clouds gliding across the sky. It wasn't until I focused on the shouts and automatic fire from the surface that I remembered why we were there.

'It is very high,' Sohail said in wonder. 'We must be a long way underground.'

'I vote we sit awhile. Can we?' I directed the question to Dr Pembley, who glanced at the passage behind him, then smiled at me.

'I don't see why not. A rest would be good, eh, son?'

Jasper only grunted.

'We could never climb that high,' Sonya lamented, gazing up at the small circle of light above. 'The walls are too smooth.'

'We shouldn't have to,' I explained. 'There'll be other passageways that lead to the surface, outside the walls, I hope.'

Sohail stalked around the curved stones, washed smooth by years of lapping water, to scout for another passageway. Jasper sank down where he stood, and leaned his head back, looking weary and pale in the dim light.

Liana and I stayed with Sonya; she seemed to want us to. I still couldn't make her out. Maybe her behaviour when we first met could be explained by her worry at being caught giving information to Mr Kumar, but her quietness in the village was strange. It could have been shyness due to the presence of Sohail's family. Looking back on it, I wondered why I never caught on there was some understanding between her and Sohail, even though they never spoke. It was the times when she said nothing or didn't look at him that gave it away.

She started the conversation, another point of interest. 'I am glad Jasper has found his father. I thought as much but I did not want to give false hope.'

'What do you mean?'

'In the beginning, when you told me about him, I thought his father might still be alive. Many European doctors have volunteered their services to help the wounded of any party or side. They are greatly respected and there are always wounded.'

'Sonya, I'm sorry about your mother being killed here. It must be difficult.'

She sighed, but it wasn't her usual irritable tone, rather that of facing the inevitable. I was surprised when she began to tell her story. 'My mother was like a princess, I was told. The family had hoped she would marry an important Afghan man. When my father wanted to marry her, Uncle Kumar's family was displeased, although they allowed it. Because of the Soviet invasion, their marriage was a great embarrassment. For you see, the war was not one of those where there were love matches or friendships struck between individuals of the two nations. Afghanistan is not like that. This country has a very harsh code of life. Death was preferable to disgrace.'

'Why—'

'My mother was seen as a traitor to her faith.'

'So you are still related to the people here in the fort?' I found it hard to believe.

'Not now. I doubt whether there are many left. Most became refugees. The fort is run by these terrorists now—always causing trouble, bombing girls' schools and taking boys from villages to fight with them. They even kill other Muslims like Sohail's father if they won't join them.'

I held my breath, not wanting to break the spell that she seemed to be under. In all the weeks we'd been together, I'd never heard her speak so much about herself.

'I only came here once. I had never been to the village until this time. I was brought up in Kabul. Even Moscow I have only seen a few times. These last two years my father has been working in the Russian Embassy in Islamabad. That was when I met Uncle Kumar in the carpet shop. He knew me; he'd kept some contact with my father. Father was always so busy that I began to spend more time with Uncle jan. I started telling him things, simple things at first.'

I didn't want to ask what those things were; I sensed she'd stop talking altogether, so I asked another question instead. 'And you hadn't met Sohail before?'

'Only when we were children. Later, he was usually at school. At times he went to Pakistan to help with the carpet business in his holidays. That is why he was there with Uncle jan this winter.'

'I wonder how we got ambushed at the waterfall.'

'It could have been Nazira.'

'But why?'

'She was jealous of me. She may have thought she would be considered to marry Sohail, and then I arrived.'

'How would she have known about us being out?'

Sonya regarded me. 'How did you know?'

'Jasper sent a note but he wrote it in English so no one would understand what it said.'

'Nazira was a good student in school. Her written English was much better than the spoken.'

'Oh.'

'It is what the war lord said to Sohail when we were being interrogated. He said someone from Sohail's household had betrayed him.'

'But if it was Nazira, she would have meant to betray you, not Sohail.'

Sonya inclined her head. I thought of the anguish she would have felt when she realised that Sohail was with us.

Then Liana said, 'I hope she confesses.'

'I, too, hope this,' Sonya said, 'Otherwise my uncle will think I am with my father. It was the plan to meet him after you had gone with your contact.'

Then I asked the question that was forming in my mind. I shouldn't have, for it broke the spell, but I couldn't help myself. 'Those carpets, the ones made in Pakistan, isn't there something strange about them? The patterns on the borders are never quite right.'

Sonya shrugged. 'It is hard to find good artists now.'

'There must be more to it than that,' I probed.

'I really could not say,' she said, and the evasion in her tone made her sound distant again, like when we first met. I realised then there were still more secrets, and maybe she would never tell them all.

We were startled as Sohail suddenly shouted, 'There are two passageways. Come and look.'

Both were as dank and evil-looking as the one we'd come from.

'How will we choose?' Sonya asked.

'Precisely.' Jasper didn't sound precise, only cautious. 'We don't want to be led back to another room.'

'It shouldn't matter.' I tried to sound confident. 'I think all the ones at Rohtas led to the surface.'

'The one we came out of didn't come from the outside.' Jasper was watching me, waiting for what I'd say next when Sonya suddenly gasped.

'What is that noise?' Her eyes widened with fear. We stood and listened. The sounds were unmistakable: heavy and fast footfalls in the passage behind us, angry and excited shouts.

'Razey! There is not the time to lose. We must go!' Sohail urged, mixing Pakhtu with his English.

Panic made Sonya's voice sound like a wail. 'Which way?'

'Throw a coin,' Jasper said.

Dr Pembley looked unconvinced but Liana pointed down the closest tunnel. 'Let's go that way.'

With the sound of the chase growing louder behind us, we quickly agreed. It was satisfying at first to find the passageway steadily rising, but it made me wish I was fitter. Soon we turned a corner and unfolding before us were hundreds of steps reaching up to the ground. When I first saw them, I wondered how Jasper would make it. They looked so steep. He leaned against the wall for a quick breather, holding his arm.

'C'mon, Jas. This is the last bit.' I paused when I saw the red oozing through his fingers but I knew it wasn't the time to make a fuss. 'You can do it, Jas,' was all I said as I started up the steps. I heard him take a deep breath to follow me, then I saw Sohail turn around to check on him. Jasper began counting the steps to keep himself going, and by the time he got to 167, it sounded as though he'd gained his second wind because he managed to keep in time with me.

'I used to do this in the dentist's chair when I was a kid,' he puffed out between steps. 'Count all the squares on the ceiling—or the fly spots—there were always so many fly spots, I never noticed the flies buzzing, only the drill ...'

That was when I screamed.

28

Jaime

I'd been willing Jasper to keep climbing and listening to his counting, so I didn't hear the step behind me. Suddenly, an arm grabbed me around my neck and I was dragged backwards. To the side I could see the angular barrel of an assault rifle held in the man's other hand. Jasper swung around the instant I screamed, took one look at me, and lunged at the man's middle. I don't know how he did that with his damaged shoulder, but it worked. The guard, none other than Vacant Eyes, dropped the gun in pained surprise and I wrenched myself free.

Jasper stooped to pick up the gun but Vacant Eyes pushed on his wounded shoulder to reach it first. Jasper gasped with the pain and we watched the gun clatter down the steps with a despairing finality. Jasper shouted at me to run. I knew why. If the guard got hold of me again, he wouldn't be tricked into letting me go a second time. With me caught, Jasper would be defenceless. I retreated further out of jumping reach.

Vacant Eyes leapt down a few steps and was reaching for the gun but Jasper followed and stunned him with a punch that made blood ooze out of the guard's nose. I knew I was supposed to be out of there, but I had to see what happened. I stood like a sparrow on a perch, almost mesmerised but ready for flight. The man threw himself at Jasper and they teetered on the step, then fell, rolling over each other with groans and grunts. Half of me wished I could help, the other half poised between gruesome awe and fear.

Jasper was bigger than Vacant Eyes, and if he had been well, he could have beaten him to a pulp, but Jasper's strength was waning. Vacant Eyes was astride him then, forcing Jasper's head down over the step and I had the fleeting impression that the guard could have broken his neck right then, but maybe the belief that Jasper was a doctor made him slower to act. That slight hesitation gave Jasper time to grope for the gun, and as Vacant Eyes tried to reach for his belt, I shouted for Sohail.

I saw the knife flash at the same time as Jasper finally pulled up the Kalashnikov with his good arm. But it didn't happen as it does in the movies; none of it did. The gun didn't even frighten Vacant Eyes. Instead, he plunged the knife down and, at the same time, took a lunge for the gun. Jasper twisted, the knife missed, but the Pakhtun's onslaught must have jarred Jasper's finger on the trigger for there was a deafening explosion and Vacant Eyes was flung backwards.

Dirt dribbled down the walls as if there'd been an earthquake. The fight must have only taken seconds as Dr Pembley and Sohail were suddenly there, picking Jasper up, while I could hear gunfire reverberating in my head.

Dazed, Jasper looked behind him. 'I didn't mean to kill him—only frighten him, to get him off me.' He was shaking.

Sohail took a swift look at Vacant Eyes sprawled on the ground. 'Do not worry, my friend. He is not dead. Put this behind you now—there are more where he came from. Come, we must hurry.' Then he picked up the gun.

Jasper and I stumbled after him. The steps were deep, the passage widening as it neared the surface. Ten men could have walked up it, side by side. That thought made me step faster, yet there was a part of me that was too weary to move. There was no doubt in my mind that Jasper had saved my life; he'd been there for me but I couldn't feel the thanks or wonder that heroines in movies show. I'd had enough of guns and the fanatical philosophy of some Afghans in the face of danger. Sohail never seemed afraid, as if it were a game—you win or lose, but hey, wasn't it fun playing? I just felt like going home.

Jasper's chest heaved and his arm bled freely no matter how hard he tried to staunch the blood with his good hand. We reached the others lying on the second step from the outside. They were staring out and I couldn't understand why they didn't flee. Surely they knew the danger. Didn't they hear the gunfire behind them?

'Why are you still here?' Jasper said between gasping breaths. 'There'll be more guys in the tunnels. We need to get out of here.' But he stopped when he saw the stunned look on his father's face.

Dr Pembley looked as though he'd landed on the moon and found it was overrun with Martians. I rushed forward to see.

The air was filled with the clamour of automatic rifle fire and the battle cry of the mujahideen. Smoke and dust drifted in, past the few shrubs that were half concealing our hiding place. I couldn't keep the panic out of my voice as my brain finally decoded what my eyes were registering.

'We're still inside the fort.'

Jasper collapsed beside me, disbelief and pain making lines on his face that he was too young to have. We were so close— only thirty metres from the outside wall. The huge ancient gate that we'd come through at night was battered, a log lying beside the splintered carved frames. That explained the pounding noise we'd heard earlier. Had the fort been attacked?

'We're near the front gate then?' No one answered me and I glanced behind us. I had visions of Vacant Eyes, dead or not, looming up behind us.

'Could we make a run for it?' I asked.

Everyone watched the Pakhtuns outside, running into the fight, long shirts flying and the tails of their turbans swinging in the action. Between the automatic fire, I heard the chanting, 'Allahu Akbar, God is great', and wondered which side He'd favour. Every man there seemed to be shouting to Him. Even the screams I heard were not from fear, just surprise at being hit.

'This is a full-scale battle!' Jasper sounded weary, but Sohail's tone was excited when he answered. 'Ji.' I almost expected him to say, 'Isn't it great?'

'My father is here, and I recognise mujahideen from the neighbouring valley. Do not fear, my father will win. He was once a great commander.'

'What about us?' Sonya took a look behind us.

Jasper was almost on his haunches, straining to see. 'We can't get caught again.'

'Yeah,' I agreed. 'Wouldn't that change the scores? If we were still hostages?'

Sohail became brisk then. Maybe he heard a noise from behind us because he began edging us out further. 'The fighting has moved down that way. If we can reach the archway, where the food stall is, across there ...'

We all nodded, ready to run. Sohail seemed to be measuring the distance to the archway and then to the wall with narrowed eyes. Then he swiftly scrutinised the fighting beyond us. 'Za, we must go. Now is our chance while the fighting has moved away from us.'

Then suddenly a shout from below us put wings to my legs. A stream of bullets whizzed past our heads as we ran towards the archway. Liana was right beside me, holding my hand as we ran when all of a sudden she fell. My hand dragged and I dropped to my knees beside her. 'Li? Get up, we have to run.' I screamed her name. 'Li!'

I heard Sohail empty the Kalashnikov into the darkness of the passageway, before he bolted after us. Liana still wasn't responding and instantly Jasper was there just as Sohail reached us. Between them they carried Liana to the archway and I ran with them.

I could only think of Liana, and if she was all right. In my mind I could see her the day I first went to boarding school. She'd been there, helping me find my under-pillow present after Mum and Dad had gone; she had held me that first night when I cried for Mum, though she was only three years older.

When we reached the safety of the archway, Dr Pembley examined her. She was pale—a trickle of blood dripped onto the ground behind her ear and the doctor was grave.

'She's alive,' was all he said, but she didn't look so alive and nobody else said a word. All my questions were drowned out by the stillness of her lying between us; even the battle didn't seem so loud.

Then Sohail shattered the calm by shouting at us to get down. 'Quickly!' And as we flattened ourselves to the ground, we saw two militants emerge from the entrance to our passageway. Not Vacant Eyes either. I glanced at the wall behind us—how on earth would we reach it without being seen?

29

Jaime

'Do you think we should make a run for the wall?' I said. 'Imagine if the fighting came this way again. We'd be right in the middle of it.'

Then I grabbed Sonya's arm. 'Isn't that your embassy car—behind the jeep?'

She followed my gaze and gaped in surprise. 'Yes, it is the official car. My father—' She rose to her knees, but Sohail pulled her down again gently, as though embarrassed to touch her.

'It is not safe,' he explained, averting his head from her as if in apology.

'But that's where we should head for,' Jasper urged.

'I know it,' returned the young Pakhtun, his voice a hiss. 'But at the right time—not now!'

Suddenly, there was even more commotion than before on the battleground. An old tank was rolling in through the gateway and turning towards the mass of men.

'That is our tank!' Sohail was jubilant as a shattering explosion tore through the air, sounds of crashing stone and screams following in its wake.

'Your tank?' If I hadn't been so worried about Liana, I would have been impressed.

'My father and his men captured it years ago.' There wasn't anything else to say. Why some government hadn't claimed it back, I didn't know, nor did I care. I just wanted to be out of there—to get Liana and Jasper to a hospital.

Jasper scanned the distance through the gate, no doubt gauging how far we'd have to run before we'd be spotted, when suddenly he froze. Sohail's shout, 'Now we go!' stirred all but Jasper to action.

'No!' Jasper was almost frantic. 'It's a trap! Get down!' We all obeyed, nerves jangling, thinking he'd seen something we hadn't. 'See that guy. There he is, standing by the car—I saw him one night. I'm sure he's the same one, Sonya. You met him. I saw you.'

With a sinking feeling, I watched Jasper's face. He looked as if he were about to accuse Sonya, just as he had done in the village, and for a moment, I couldn't work out why he was worrying about incidentals when Liana was lying so still on the ground. Then I realised he was in his 'I've got to save everyone' mode again. He'd been close to Liana too, and seeing her shot would have affected him more than he showed.

Sonya took one look at the car and smiled back at Jasper.

'It is my father, Jasper. He is here for us. Yes, I met him one night, but he came to help us escape. I was to join him, since you had your route worked out. I even had the horse hidden, ready to go when we were at the waterfall, but then we were ambushed.'

Jasper tried to grin. I felt sorry for him having to eat humble pie like that. 'You did your best, Jas. There's no need to do any 'more.' No one else would have understood the clumsy words I was saying, but I think Jasper did, for he seemed to relax.

Another explosion from the tank caused more stone from the fort to fall.

'Now! Let us go!' Sohail cut in suddenly. No one from the fighting seemed to notice our dash to the wall, nor our creeping along in single file to the gaping hole that once held an ancient gate. Jasper carried the empty Kalashnikov for appearances' sake, while Sohail brought up the rear more slowly, carrying Liana.

Sonya's father saw his daughter first and, with evident relief, folded her in his arms and murmured endearments that only she could understand. Sohail took Liana to the limousine and laid her on the back seat. He stood and greeted Sonya's father formally.

I was just wondering when they would start rushing Liana and Jasper to the hospital when suddenly Sohail staggered backwards as a body launched itself at him. I screamed as I recognised the shalwar qameez of one of the militants. Before anyone could move, the bigger man had Sohail by the scruff of the neck and pulled him up, face-to-face, his turban knocked off in the scuffle. Too late, I remembered the rifle Jasper had won in the tunnel was empty.

Then my eyes watered as the bearded man spoke. 'What do you think you're doing, mate?'

I couldn't contain myself a moment longer. I sobbed as I hurled myself at the man. All I wanted was to be safe in his arms.

'Dad! I thought you were a militant.' Then I remembered Sohail. 'Let him go, Dad, it's okay—this is Sohail. He helped us and he's our friend.'

When I said those words, Sohail glanced down at me and in that moment, I knew I'd spoken the truth.

Dad was confused as he took his hands off Sohail. 'I'm sorry, mate, but you must know how it looked. And I've been so worried.' He reached for me then, and hugged me so hard I thought my ribs might pop. 'I didn't recognise you either, sunshine.'

Sohail grinned through the dirt on his face. 'I am not offended, sahib. We are just happy to be alive.'

Then I saw Uncle Jon—so that was how Dad got there.

'It's all over.' He came striding over. 'The fort has surrendered and negotiations are in process for a calmer relationship between the villages in this area. I might see the buildings that I helped build stay up from now on.'

'I must show myself to my father,' Sohail said. 'It may make some difference to the proceedings.' His eyes twinkled at us and I watched him go with a heaviness that wasn't only because of Liana. Sohail made me think of honour and strength in the face of insurmountable obstacles. Maybe if there were more guys like him, Afghanistan would find true freedom.

Dad was bending over Liana then, asking how she was.

'She's still alive,' was all Dr Pembley said.

At the words, Dad swung round. 'Stagger me! I know that voice—Joe, Joe Pembley! Heard you were dead, mate.' He grasped Dr Pembley to himself. 'So you were holed up here—all this time?'

Dr Pembley stepped back and grinned. 'Yeah, and I have Jasper to thank for my escape. If he hadn't stepped in the path of a bullet, I would never have known the kids were even in the fort.'

Dad was standing in front of Jasper then. He was looking at the wounded shoulder, still bleeding, and the fatigue etched into Jasper's dirt-streaked face.

'No doubt I have you to thank for the safety of my daughter, Jasper.' He didn't say any more, and he glanced at Liana, lying in the back of the car. It was as though he was saying, 'Thanks, I didn't expect any of you alive and well'; as if Jasper's shoulder and Liana's head wound were good odds.

It was small consolation to me.

اللہ

Getting Liana out of Afghanistan to Peshawar took longer than our trip into the country did. All the check posts that we had missed going in suddenly sprang up like rabbit traps on our way out. Fortunately, Uncle Jon was there. Everyone seemed to know him, unless he was just very clever with his Pakhtu.

The Peshawar Public Hospital didn't look promising. The waiting line was very long, even though it was well into the evening. Uncle Jon and Dr Pembley kept trying to get the man at the front desk to let us through. 'Emergency, emergency,' they kept saying. Weird how the most important words are the same in every language. Dr Pembley even shouted at people; he knew more than us, knew the danger of head wounds and how long people could survive being unconscious like that. Uncle Jon produced money, lots of it.

'Everything is emergency here.' The man at the desk sounded harassed, as if he really needed the money but there was truly nothing he could do. 'Please understand. Here, everyone is shot. You must wait.'

Then there were the forms and the proof of identification. Do you think any of us had any? Jasper sat with his good arm around me, calm for once, and looking as miserable as I felt.

Finally, a doctor came to give Liana a preliminary examination. We'd been there three hours. After a cursory check, the inevitable showed in his features. 'We cannot help,' he said. Just like that. No 'sorry', no explaining, just 'we cannot help'.

'Don't you have any facilities at all for surgery like this?' Dr Pembley's face was grey and I glanced away from the fear showing so naked on his face.

'We have no facilities—not for this. These cases always die. They never regain consciousness, you understand.'

'But if the pressure is released ...'

'We must help those who have the best chance. We don't have time to waste—maybe a hospital in Islamabad?'

Another three-and-a-half-hour drive? That was when I truly despaired. Even a plane would take too long to hire, haggling over the price, the getting from the airport to the hospital. I buried my head in Jasper's shirt and felt Dad's hand on my arm.

'We'll take the embassy car,' Dr Pembley said suddenly, brisk again, once he'd realised nothing could be done. Sonya's father had stayed in the village with Mr Kumar but he'd allowed us to take Aslam and the car with written authority, in case we were stopped. I was never so glad of Aslam's fast driving as I was then, while I sat in the back with Liana's head in my lap. I talked to her as if she could hear me. I told her all sorts of things—what it's like in Australia now, since she hadn't seen it for years; about Danny, how I made friends with him last year at school; and Blake. I even tried to tell her how hilarious Kate Sample was when she thought I was acting like a nerd, except I couldn't make anything sound funny. That was when I decided that however hard it was, I'd write Liana's story—the one she told me in the village just before we escaped. I was the only one who knew it all, besides Mr Kimberley.

The hospital in Islamabad was an improvement but no one rushed out to help with a stretcher and oxygen. And there was also the inevitable red tape and waiting line, though not as long.

Dad and I took a room in a hotel nearby (one with a TV for Dad to watch the cricket). I could never concentrate long enough to get interested. Dad was impressed with David Warner and Steve Smith: 'What a display of powerful hitting, perfect timing'. He was trying to take my mind off Liana but, even when Dad said the series was finished and the match was a tie, I was unmoved, and just thought how pleased Sohail would be that we hadn't won.

Every afternoon Dad took me to see Liana. When Mr Kimberley wasn't there, I sat and held her hand and told her about dancing in the woods and the fun we'd had all through school but there was never any change. Her olive skin was pale; her eyelids transparent as though she had already left. When the hospital rang us on the sixth morning to come in, I knew.

I'd dealt with the possibility that Jasper could die in the fort—all of us really, but not Liana. I had hoped she was safe with in the village. Maybe she was the one out of all of us most at peace to die, but I didn't want to accept that then. All I could see was how things didn't turn out the way I wanted.

Maybe unrealistic expectations make an outcome hurt so much. Was it so naïve to hope we'd all survive?

Mr Kimberley was a mess, yet he managed to spend some time with me, and still managed to whisper, 'Don't give up hope, don't despair.' Maybe it was because he was older, had been through more, which enabled him to say that; or was it because he was so like Liana? She would have believed his words. It shocked me enough to think what he must have been feeling, and enough to remember that the enchantment that was Liana would never die. I think he felt it too, for that was when he began talking of her; about that time of crisis during the terrorist attack years ago when I was taken hostage with the others, when he and Liana saved our lives.

It helped, a little.

30

Jaime

We buried Liana in the little garden near the school with all the kids and babies who had died from cholera and typhoid during the British Raj, and with Jeremy, Carolyn's brother. If you stood right where Liana's grave was, you could see the Kashmir Mountains and the Hindu Kush through the pines, rolling into one huge mountain range. It was like a 360-degree panoramic photograph; so beautiful, it didn't seem real. Liana would have loved it but I knew she wasn't there any more. The view was just for us and for her memory.

Dad and I packed that afternoon, ready to catch a flight in a few days. He said there wasn't a great deal of urgency since I was already late to start Year 12; I may as well get myself together first. He meant the reaction to the kidnapping and Liana, but that afternoon I felt fine—I guessed I was numb.

The day before Dad and I were to leave, Mr Kumar came to the school. When Carolyn rushed into the room to let me know Dad and I had a visitor, I felt the stirrings of the same childish excitement I'd have before a trip to the mountains as a kid. I was surprised as I didn't think I'd ever feel like that again. I didn't dare hope it was Sohail or his father for that would be too unusual, but who else could it be? I hurried down the two flights of stairs, pulled my long top over my jeans and knocked on the staffroom door.

Dad and Dr Pembley were already in there, and I knew that Mr Kumar was, too, before I saw him. He had a kind of presence that you could almost touch; the whole staffroom was filled with him and once you saw him, there was nowhere else to look.

'Assalamu Alaikum, May God's peace be upon you,' I greeted formally.

'Wa Alaikum Assalam,' he returned, bowing his turbaned head slightly, his arm across his chest in a humble gesture of greeting. 'It is good to see the daughter of Wayne Sahib again.' Then he smiled, managing not to look at me directly, yet I knew the smile was just for me. 'I am very sorry to hear of Misahiba Liana's passing and bring affsos from my whole family. We feel the heavy responsibility of her death.'

'Shukriya, thank you.'

'I was very impressed with her noble ways. You must have loved her greatly.'

'Yes.'

'Now, I have brought you an invitation and a gift.'

'How kind.' Even though I kept my voice sounding formal and subdued, I could feel a stirring inside me again. How like the people of that part of the world—condolences for a death in one breath, an invitation to life in the next.

'But first, I want to see the son of the Doctor Sahib. Is this possible?'

I rang the boys' hostel, and in the meantime, tea arrived for the Mr Kumar from the dining room. I tried to serve him in the style he would be used to. Soon Jasper arrived, puffing slightly, his dark hair ruffled and his left arm in a sling. He greeted the great man properly and with obvious pleasure. I couldn't help thinking what a change it was from the first time we were imprisoned in the carpet shop in Peshawar.

The Pakhtun stood and, after the customary hug that only occurred between members of the same sex, held Jasper at arm's length, scrutinising him. Then he sighed as if what he saw pleased him. 'I see you have come to terms with yourself and life at last, beta. Peace is written on your face where before it was not.'

Jasper nodded. 'Yes, sir—and I want to say thank you for all you tried to do for me—Sohail too. I'm sorry. I didn't realise your ... position.' Jasper's voice faltered and died away but the Pakhtun's smile was huge.

'You truly are the son of your father. There was a time I wasn't so sure, but a man who can admit his wrongs is a great one indeed.'

Dr Pembley coughed and I felt sorry for Jasper. How embarrassing for him having all those things said when we were within earshot.

'Come.' Mr Kumar moved to where some long bundles lay on the carpet. Swiftly, expertly, he unrolled two large prayer rugs. The third he left rolled. He was pleased with himself in a contained sort of way, and I tried to enter into his mood. I didn't have to pretend for the rugs were excellent. I looked down on the bottom border of one. The pattern was lovely, perfect, except for—there it was again. I bent down for a closer look.

'Ahh,' exclaimed Mr Kumar and he didn't sound displeased. 'Your daughter is very intelligent,' he offered to Dad. Then he turned to me. 'Well, what do you see, beti? Tell me.'

I felt I needed to be careful. These were a gift, they might have been his best, and what if I were wrong about the patterns being changed? To say a carpet was badly made would be a terrible insult. Mr Kumar was watching me. 'Your "brother" also saw something that night in my office.' I looked across at Jasper. It just seemed too much of a coincidence for them all to be the result of poor workmanship.

'The pattern is fine here—' I pointed to the lower border '—and here. It's like the ones in your home. We both noticed it. I don't mean to be offensive but they always seem to have bigger differences than the usual mistake or two that can occur.' There, I'd said it. I waited for the storm to break.

'Look closer, beti.'

Surprised, I crouched on my hands and knees to examine the carpet. I thought he'd be upset, but here he was, inviting us to make a comment on his gift. Then suddenly, I gasped. 'There's something here ... English letters! Between the flowers on the border.' I tried to spell them out, 'I-L-S-O-N-Y, no, SOHAIL—SONYA—March 17.' I looked up. 'That's only next month.' I was still forming the idea in my mind, hoping.

'It is an invitation, beti.'

I was right. 'To Sohail and Sonya's wedding?'

'Ji, a shadi invitation.' The excitement I felt at being invited suddenly fizzled like a wet firecracker when I realised I wouldn't be there. The next day I would leave. It's strange how in such a short time you can feel so much a part of a person's life that you want to share their special moments with them. Why is life so full of heartbreaking choices and decisions? I think in that second, if they'd begged me, I would have stayed and said, 'stuff Year 12 and my university education'.

I caught Jasper's glance on me, and I realised Mr Kumar was talking again. 'And there is a special request, Jasper. Sohail wishes to pass over his distinguished blood relatives and have you as witness at his wedding.'

'He—what?' Jasper wasn't the only one astonished. I'd never heard anything like that happening before. 'Zarur, certainly I'd be honoured,' Jasper managed to say.

Mr Kumar smiled through his beard. 'I think this shadi will be somewhat different to others in our family of late.'

'Mr Kumar? Is Sonya well?' Believe it or not, during our time in the fort I became fond of Sonya. I realised she had the good of Afghanistan at heart and would do all she could to help a country that most of the world didn't seem to care about. 'We were worried what might happen to her.'

The commander moved to the couch and motioned for us also to sit. 'Sonya is well, Allah be praised. Due to her youth, her father has managed to negotiate with the Russian intelligence to drop charges on the understanding that he resigns his post in the embassy. Having their agent in our storeroom helped in this matter a great deal.' His eyes twinkled under his bushy brows.

I was surprised that it really was a Russian agent who was after Sonya. I thought that sort of thing would have stopped years ago when the Union broke up. I guess there'd be many countries which didn't want a unified government in Afghanistan and so the fighting and intrigue goes on, and the wall of silence rises higher.

'They suggested also, in order to keep her out of trouble, to marry her to a handsome, young freedom fighter and leave her in the mountains. Which is exactly what will happen.

Sohail and Sonya will live at the fort and Sohail will be its new commander.'

'Wild!' I whispered.

'They have plans to rebuild and make it a village of social reform.' He turned to Dad. 'Sohail has already been talking to your English friend, Jon Harris, about these things.'

He turned back to Jasper and me. 'I am sorry you cannot come to Afghanistan for a while. I have had much trouble with the authorities for taking you across the border in the first place, but most of the wedding festivities will be held in Peshawar, and we shall be honoured by your presence there.'

I tried to look as happy as Jasper. Then Mr Kumar gestured to the carpets spread on the floor. 'These are a gift from us. You will each find your name woven on one.' I knew then who the third one was for. 'The English writing included in the weave was Sonya's wish. She said you would appreciate it very much.'

I stared at Jasper. Was he thinking what I was? That this was Sonya's way of telling us the secret at last? I had to know.

'Mr Kumar?' I appealed. 'May I ask a question?'

'Zarur, most certainly.'

'Is this why the patterns on the carpets in your house were different? I mean, these have a story, a secret to tell just for us. Was that how you got messages back into Afghanistan after Sonya told you information? You had carpets on the looms in the camps all ready, except for the last few centimetres where you had the message woven in?'

Mr Kumar chuckled. I couldn't tell what he was thinking, nor did he speak. Jasper had caught onto what I meant. 'Did you do that in the village too? I saw your carpet factory. They said you provided the patterns. If at any time you needed to get a message to Peshawar, to party headquarters—is that how you did it?'

Mr Kumar regarded Jasper for so long that I wondered if we'd gone too far. Maybe he'd never guessed that we knew as much as we did. Yet, I quietly added, 'And we couldn't work out any of it because the symbols and letters were in Persian?'

The great Pakhtun chuckled again, and I saw Jasper breathe easier.

'I think you had a good try though, beti.'

'So ... it's true?'

He stroked his beard while we waited.

'Now, I cannot help it if I have lazy workers who make the rugs poorly in the refugee camps.'

I heard Dad's low laugh, and I wanted to ask Mr Kumar again but he stood up.

'May I have your permission to leave?' He seemed to be asking me and I didn't know whether to refuse the customary three times or not. I glanced at Jasper, but finally we just nodded dumbly, sorry to see the visit finished so soon.

After the ritualistic salaams and goodbyes, Mr Kumar turned before getting into his van and faced us, his arm crossed over his chest. 'I want to thank you from my heart. Allah has been good to us—you have done more in my family and community than you know. I think, also, I can trust you to keep this ... surmising of yours ... a secret?' I thought his smile at that moment was maddening—as though there was so much more to know. 'You may certainly think what you will. I shall not deny you that—but more? I cannot tell you. Goodbye, children. Manda na bashi, may you never be tired.'

'And may you live long,' we responded. We stood there,

watching his van drive out of the school gates. I felt as if he and his family were driving out of my life forever, and something special would always be missing.

'Why do you think he wouldn't tell us?' I finally asked Jasper. 'Too dangerous?'

'It's obvious,' Jasper said. 'If he told us, it wouldn't be a secret any more.' I guessed he was right. Nothing is straightforward in that part of the world. There is always the element of things not as they seem. Even what people say is not always true in the way people in the West understand truth.

Jasper turned to me then. 'I saw your face when we got the wedding invite. I'm sorry. Guess it'd be too much to ask you to stay longer.'

'I have to go now or it will be too difficult.' I didn't know how to explain it, but if I returned to Pakistan when I was older, I wanted it to be because I chose to, not because I couldn't find my place in Australia and was always yearning for somewhere else.

'I understand.' He reached into his pocket. 'I have something for you. I was going to give it to you tomorrow, but tomorrow will be difficult enough.'

'Jas, why is it so hard to say goodbye? You'd think we'd be used to it, growing up the way we have, away from our home countries, but each time I say it, it gets worse. The older I get, the more things I know I'll miss.'

'There is one thing, Jaime—the world has a habit of getting smaller each time you cross it. People you never thought you'd see again, you do.' He grinned, although he didn't look happy. 'You'll be back. I can see you as an aid worker or a journalist, tramping around countries like Afghanistan with the UN.'

He gave me the box then. When I opened it, I was so moved I couldn't speak. For a moment, I thought it was the one he sold to get the horses, and I took it out to try it on. How did he get the money to buy me a gold bangle?

'Wait.' He took it from me. 'I want to put it on. It's not the original one, but it's truly close.' He was pleased I liked it, and I was touched that he'd taken enough notice of my other one to have it copied in the bazaar. His eyes were bright and he took my hands in his, as he did that day in the village.

'Jaime, will there be a friend for you when you get back? Not too many people would understand what you've just been through, let alone believe it.' Didn't I know it! There was so much I'd never told people in Australia for fear they'd never relate to it, or would think I was making it up. Yasmeen would understand. Not many of the kids from school would, though. My friend Danny would try. Then there was Blake. He'd said to make sure I came back.

'Yes, I think there's someone.' By the way Jasper looked at me, he knew I was thinking of a guy.

'I'm glad,' was all he said and I believed he meant it. How could he be everything that I needed fifteen thousand kilometres away? I stood there staring at him, wanting to remember everything about him.

'What about you? Will you be okay?'

'Jaime, when Li died…' my eyes watered; I found it hard to listen to that phrase. '… I knew that what I went through last year—not knowing if Dad was dead or alive—wasn't for nothing. I know that's no help to you, but Jaime, I love your hope, the way you don't give up. Please don't lose that when things don't turn out.' He looked embarrassed, as though he had no right to say that after the way he'd handled his own grief, but maybe that's why he could. Maybe that's why we go through anything: to pass on what we've learnt.

I smiled, even though my eyes were blurry. Now and then you find a friend who touches a place deep inside you and you know that in another time or place, something special would have happened. Jasper was like that but I knew this wasn't the time. It was as though Jasper was following my thoughts, for the brightness in his eyes spilled out and ran down his cheek, yet he kept holding my hand. 'This time we'll write, okay?' And he kissed me one last time.

As I stepped onto the tarmac the next day, I made sure I said goodbye. I turned around and waved to all of Pakistan: its magic and mystery, its fanaticism and friendliness, its cruelty and kindness, and—Liana. It must have looked weird but I had to do it. I was laying the ghosts to rest that had beckoned to me all through the last year in Australia, whispering, 'Come back, you don't belong there.'

I had made Pakistan into something in my memory that wasn't altogether true and if I hadn't gone back, I would never have known; I'd always be wishing and longing for someplace else. Now I can look ahead to the next step. Maybe it won't always be exciting but I found that even a place like Pakistan only appears like that from ten thousand kilometres away.

Kate Sample wasn't totally right; Pakistan hadn't changed so much, but another thing had, and that was me. I could see two worlds more clearly now and I would try to adjust, accepting their differences while not losing mine, as I walked with thanks beyond their borders.

Acknowledgements

I wish to thank journalist Ken Packer for his invaluable help with this manuscript when I was learning how to write in point of view. Thank you to Rhiza Press who had faith in me to rewrite this adventure.

The words Sohail quotes are from Rumi, excerpt from "The War Inside," translated by Kabir Helminski, from *Love is a Stranger*, © 1993 by Kabir Edmund Helminski. Reprinted by arrangement with The Permissions Company, Inc., on behalf of Shambhala Publications Inc., Boulder, CO. www.shambhala.com.

Word List

(Words are from the Urdu unless otherwise stated)

abu	dad
accha	good
affsos	condolences
afghani	Afghan paper money (Dari)
Allah	God (Arabic)
Allahu Akbar	God is great (Arabic)
Angrez	English person/s
Assalamu Alaikum	God's peace be upon you, hello (Arabic)
azan	call to prayer
bazaar	market
beta	son
beti	daughter
burqa	a cover all for women
chai	tea, often milky and sweet
chapatti	flat bread
charpai	stringed wooden bed
chello	move
chowkidar	nightwatchman
Dari	national language of Afghanistan
dupatta	long scarf
emir	king
gali	small alley way or lane
hakim	doctor
halal	permissible
Inglestan	England
Isa	Jesus (Arabic)
jaldi	quickly

jan	life, used after a name as a form of endearment
ji	yes, or used after a name as a term of respect
jirga	tribal council
Kalashnikov AK 47	30 shot round automatic assault rifle
khan	leader/chief/commander
Khuda	God
khush amdeed	welcome
kissah kahani	street of storytellers in Peshawar
missahiba	miss
mujahid, mujahedeen (p)	those who fight a jihad or freedom fighter/s
mullah	priest
naan	flat bread made with yeast
nay	no (slang)
Pakhtu	language of the Pakhtuns
Pakhtun	ethnic group of Afghanistan
pilau	rice dish
poshteen	sheepskin vest
purdah	separation from men than women observe
qameez	long shirt
rabaab	stringed musical instrument like a sitar
Ramadan	Muslim month of fasting
raza /razey	come (Pakhtu)
rupee	unit of money
rumal	handkerchief
Ruse	Russia
salaam	hello, peace

samovar	ancient water heating urn
shadi	wedding
shalwar qameez	suit of clothes
shalwar	long baggy pants
shareef	noble
shukriya	thank you
sunno	listen
tabla	hand drum
tandoor	clay oven
tonga	horse-drawn carriage
Urdu	national language of Pakistan
Wa Alaikum Assalam	and peace be upon you (Arabic)
za	go (Pakhtu)
zarur	certainly

More from Rosanne Hawke

Beyond Borders : Dear Pakistan

Jaime Richards has spent most of her life in Pakistan and returning to Australia seems like another planet compared to the country she has left behind. Here in Australia, boys try to kiss her, men wear shorts and everyone says 'cool' all the time. How will she ever know the right things to say or do or wear? After all, this is meant to be her culture.

This is a story of living beyond borders, and discovering the gift of adapting to new cultures, especially one's own.

Beyond Borders : Liana's Dance

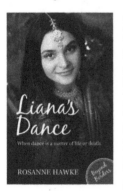

After her international high school in Northern Pakistan is attacked by terrorists, sixteen-year-old Liana Bedford and the young music and dance teacher, Mikal Kimberley must find a way to rescue student hostages who have been imprisoned in an ancient caravanserai. Liana discovers Mikal Kimberley has a secret and to save him and her friends she must overcome her fears and dance for her life.

This is Liana's story as told by her friend Jaime Richards from *Dear Pakistan* and *The War Within*.

About the Author

Rosanne Hawke is a South Australian author of over 25 books, among them, *Zenna Dare*, *Mustara*, shortlisted in the 2007 NSW Premier's Literary Awards, *The Messenger Bird*, winner of the 2013 Cornish Holyer an Gof Award for YA literature, and *Taj and the Great Camel Trek*, winner of the 2012 Adelaide Festival awards. Rosanne was an aid worker in Pakistan and the United Arab Emirates for ten years and now teaches creative writing at Tabor Adelaide. In 2015 she was the recipient of the Nance Donkin Award for an Australian woman author who writes for children and YA.